SWEET REWARDS

LORI BEASLEY BRADLEY

❁ I ❁

Olivia Thibodeaux Montgomery sat on the veranda outside her second-floor bedroom at her father's home and watched jagged forks of the lightning spear the sky to the west. She hoped a late spring storm would do something to diminish the oppressive heat. She fanned herself vigorously as Magdalena, her maid, friend, confidant, and her blood half-sister, brushed her raven hair up off her porcelain-skinned neck to twist into a tight bun on the top of her head.

"If it rains," Olivia asked, fanning away a petulant mosquito, "do you think Daddy will call off this horrid party tonight?" Since the loss of her husband, William Montgomery, at Vicksburg in a violent clash between Union and Confederate troops, Olivia had resumed residing with her parents on their palatial sugar plantation, Sweet Rewards, west of New Orleans. Her father spent lavish amounts of money on parties trying to lure suitors for Olivia's hand in marriage. Armand Thibodeaux was desperate for a male heir to Sweet Rewards that only Olivia could give him now that her mother was in her late forties and past her childbearing years.

"Daddy ain't gonna cancel this party, Miss Livvy. He bettin' the farm on this riverboat man catchin' your fancy. He done brung him all the way out here from St. Louis to meet up with y'all."

"Magda, don't go calling me Miss Livvy here in my own room. You know I don't hold with that old slave nonsense. You are not my slave. You are my sister, and everyone in this God-forsaken Parish knows it."

"That may be, but Daddy still do, and if he heared me callin' you anything but Miss Livvy, he'd be whoopin' my black ass for sure."

"Yes, but Daddy isn't in my bedroom at this minute, and your ass is about as black as mine." She jerked her head and yelped when one of Magdalena's pins stabbed her scalp. "You did that on purpose, and you can stop talkin' like an uneducated cane-field nigger. You had the same tutors I did and can speak better than I do most of the time."

"I most certainly can, but I did not do that on purpose. You won't hold still." Magda laughed. "I may be an educated house nigger, but Daddy isn't out there looking for some rich riverboat man for me to marry, is he? He'll marry me up with one of them dumb cane-field niggers of his and call it good."

"He will not," Olivia protested, "you are a free woman and can marry any man you please. Daddy can't force you to marry anyone you don't want to anymore."

"You mean like he can't force you to marry up with no rich riverboat man?" Magda snorted indignantly. "He still treats me like a house slave. He made me bed with that fat old bastard Remus last week when he was here."

Olivia stood and jerked the tie of her dressing gown tight at the waist in anger. "Why didn't you come to me, Magda? I would have put a stop to that nonsense. He's got no right to do that. You have not been a slave for almost ten years now."

"It's alright, Livvy." Magdalena walked to the wrought-iron railing around the veranda to try and catch a cooling breeze. She ran a hand the color of heavily creamed coffee over her black hair, twisted into a tight bun at the back of her neck, and wrapped with a cotton cloth, denoting her place as a house servant. "Mammy says that if I'm nice to Remus, he might ask her to come work for him, and she'd like that. She loves your mother, but she's gettin' too old to put up with Daddy's depravities anymore. Anyhow, old Remus just rolls over and goes to sleep after I suck his little cock."

"Magda, don't be crude," Olivia chided and then asked with a giggle, "Is it really all that little?"

Magdalena stuck her thumb into the air and smiled. "Not much bigger than this. With that belly of his, I bet he ain't been able to see it in years unless he's in front of a mirror."

Olivia giggled along with her sister.

She took Olivia's hand and tugged her toward the bedroom. "Come on in now, and let's get you into the bath. Daddy's going to want you smellin' all fresh and sweet for tonight." They went through the glass-paned French doors into Olivia's opulent bedroom, where a servant had filled her white enameled tub with hot water.

"What am I wearing to this little circus tonight?" Olivia asked as she dropped her dressing gown to the floor, revealing a tall, slim body with raven hair falling nearly to her shapely behind. She stepped gingerly into the tub, testing the water's temperature with her toes before climbing in and sitting.

"I think you should wear that new orchid gown

your mother brought back from N'Orleans last month. It is so pretty and looks just like one I saw in a color plate of Empress Josephine. Nobody wears that old-style anymore, and the color is almost the same as your eyes. I'm sure it will impress that river-boat man." Magdalena went to the wardrobe and brought out the orchid silk-chiffon dress with its high empire waist and short puffed sleeves. She laid it out across the bed and went on to pull clean undergar-ments from the heavy oak bureau.

"I'm gonna fix that pretty little diamond tiara in your hair and," Magdalena went on pulling things from the bureau drawers, "this diamond choker and dangling earbobs. You will look just like a princess from the court in France."

"I'm certain that is exactly what this man is looking for," Olivia sighed as she squeezed warm water from a sea sponge over her face to run down her throat and over her pale white breasts, "a planta-tion princess with two hundred acres of cane fields *and* a processing plant for sugar."

"What difference does that make if he can give you the babies Mr. William couldn't?"

Olivia thought of her sweet William and how their hopes had been dashed every month when her flux had come. "I don't think it was William's fault. I'm the only living child Mother ever bore. Daddy says she comes from bad blood. Maybe I'm the same. William and I were married for two years before he went off to the war, and I never conceived once."

"Livvy, you were young. Lots of girls don't con-ceive until they get into their twenties. You are twenty-four now, and maybe this riverboat man will have a huge set of ballocks to make lots of good strong seed. Mr. William, he was a small man. Did he have small ballocks too?"

Olivia's face flushed in her tub. William's were the only human ballocks she had ever seen. She had no idea if they were big, small, or otherwise. She knew Magdalena had much more experience with men than she did, having been passed around to her father's friends on many occasions and having had dalliances with young men on the plantation over the years.

"I am quite certain William's ballocks were more than sufficient for the task." She stood and pulled a large cotton towel from a brass hook on the wall and wrapped herself in it before stepping out onto the long, oval, braided rug.

They both gave a start when someone tapped on the door. Olivia pulled the towel tight around her as her mother came into the room from the hall, aided by her silver-handled cane to walk. Marie Thibodeaux saw the orchid dress lying out on the bed and smiled.

"Thank you for choosing that one, Olivia. Your father will be ever so pleased." Marie picked up the dress and held it up, admiring the soft, ethereal fabric that fluttered in the breeze coming through the open French doors from the veranda.

"Thank Magda," Olivia told her mother bluntly. "It is not what I would have chosen."

"I'm not gonna let her wear another one of them old black dresses to any of her father's parties no more, ma'am," Magdalena declared, giving Olivia a petulant grin.

"Thank *you* then, Magdalena." Maria laid the dress back onto the bed. "Would you mind giving Olivia and me some time alone, dear?"

"Of course not, ma'am." Magdalena gave Marie a quick curtsey and left the room.

"Olivia, William has been gone for seven years

now. It's time for you to move on with your life." Marie rested her frail frame on the bed and leaned her cane next to her. "I was hopeful when you took off your mourning clothes two years ago, but you have spurned the advances of every man your father has presented to you since."

"Mother, no man will ever be able to replace William in my heart. His grasp on it is still strong. I can think of no other." Olivia's gaze fell on the silver-framed photo resting upon her nightstand of the man in a starched gray captain's uniform of the Confederate Calvary. The image was all in muted tones of black and gray, but Olivia swore she could see the bright blue twinkle in those silent, fixed eyes.

"*Ma Cherie*." Marie took her daughter's hand. "I know you loved William very much, and he loved you very much too. That is something most women never experience in a lifetime. You are a very lucky woman, but it is time to carry on with your life and find another to father your children."

And there it is. The reason Father wants me to marry. All he cares about is a male heir for Sweet Rewards. I'm nothing more than a damned broodmare, in his opinion.

"Tell me, Mother, is this man a friend of Father's with all of his same distasteful proclivities? Does he frequent whores and abuse women for the fun of it?"

Marie reached to touch the silver handle of the cane at her side. "Your father was not always the man he is now. We come from different times, Olivia. Your father and I had our slaves and our French culture. Armand was an extremely handsome young man, and I was overwhelmed by his charms and that he chose to ask for my hand out of all the debutants presented that year." Marie sighed sadly and took a deep breath. "Then he was involved in that foolish duel that scarred his face, and he changed. Your father is a vain man, and the loss of his looks affected him more than I could ever have thought. In the end, he blamed me because he'd called the man out for insulting my virtue. Then when I failed to provide him with a living male child to carry on the Thibodeaux name, he blamed me again."

"Mother, none of that was *your* fault," Olivia protested to her sad mother. "Father had no business calling out a man to duel with blades when he didn't have the skill to do so, and women lose children out here in this miserable swamp all the time. He should have taken you into New Orleans, where there are good doctors and midwives. He should have taken you to the townhouse in the city instead of leaving you out here in this filthy swamp."

"I had good care here, Olivia. Georgia took very good care of me, just like Magdalena takes good care of you." Marie stood and hobbled with her cane out onto the veranda, where a cool wind had picked up, blowing clouds heavy with rain up from the Gulf. Olivia bit her lip and followed her mother. "New Orleans in the summer is a terrible place to be. It is hot and has miasmas. Yellow fever takes hundreds every year. Sweet Rewards was the only place I ever wanted to be during my pregnancies."

"So tell me about this man Father has chosen for me to marry this time," Olivia said, changing the subject. "Have you met him?"

"We have dined with him on occasion in New Orleans. He is quite handsome and owns a shipping line on the Mississippi and Ohio Rivers. He has offices in New Orleans, but his main office and home are in St. Louis, I believe."

"Why has he not married already? Is he widowed, or does he simply prefer paid women in his bed?"

"There is no need to be crude, Olivia Marie. From what I have seen of him, he is a hard-working man who has put many years into building up his business on the rivers. I think he has simply chosen to wait until he could offer a woman security before looking to marry. I think that is commendable."

"I think he is simply looking to add a sugar plantation and a processing plant to his holdings by marrying the widowed daughter of the plantation's owner," Olivia sneered.

"Olivia, I could not give your father a proper heir to Sweet Rewards, so that responsibility now falls upon you." Marie limped back into the room and sat upon the chaise lounge by the doors where she could enjoy the breeze while watching her daughter dress.

"Mother," Olivia dropped her dressing gown on the bed and began pulling on her bloomers. "I will not make you any promises, but I will meet this man and listen to what he has to say."

"I cannot ask for more, *Cherie*. Your father will be ever so very pleased." Marie took her daughter's hand again and smiled. "And I am very pleased about the dress and the tiara. Make certain you wear the white opera gloves with it. You will look *tres chic, ma petite*. You will look just like Josephine herself in all her royal splendor."

❦ 2 ❧

F rom her room, Olivia could hear the noise rising from the parlor below. The orchestra warmed up, and the knocking at the door announced new arrivals to the night's soiree. Magdalena fussed over her, fitting the tiara perfectly straight upon Olivia's head, and slapped her shoulder every time she fidgeted in the chair.

"Will you please hold still, Livvy? I want to get this pinned in nice an' tight, so it doesn't go slidin' off your hard head into the punch bowl."

Olivia let her sister have her way and sat perfectly still. They heard another knock on the door from below. "Do you think that might be him?" Olivia asked with a twinge of nervous energy. "The orchestra won't begin to play until he gets here. Then I can make my grand appearance on the stairs."

"You're going to take that rich riverboat man's breath plum away, Livvy." She patted the diamond choker down flat around Olivia's white throat. When they heard the orchestra, she pulled Olivia to her feet. "Now, walk carefully, so you don't knock that tiara off."

"How can I possibly when you have it tacked to my skull with horseshoe nails?"

From the top of the stairs, Olivia could see the regular swamp-rat gentry from the neighboring plantations. They never passed up an opportunity to show off their Paris fashions ordered from the shops in New Orleans. The women wore the slimmer skirts with all the frilled aprons and ridiculous big bows on their backsides. They simply couldn't pass up the free food and drink offered by her father on these occasions, and it irritated Olivia to no end.

Between her parents stood a tall man in an elegant black silk waistcoat, trousers, and top hat. He stood almost a head taller than her six-foot-tall father, and his tanned face was extremely handsome in a rakish sort of way. Above his full lips, he wore a pencil-thin mustache, and his eyes were slate-blue like the tiles on their townhouse in New Orleans. They weren't a bright, sparkling, playful blue like William's had been but a darker, smoldering, brooding blue, giving him an air of coldness, distance, and mystery. His broad shoulders were well-defined in the jacket and his waist trim in the perfectly pressed trousers. Although this man was easily ten years her senior, Olivia found he aroused her.

Perhaps Mother is right. Seven years without a man between my legs has been long enough.

Olivia was happy for the confining corset because thinking about being with the man had caused her nipples to harden and become erect under the heavy brocade fabric. It also embarrassed her to admit to the throbbing between her thighs and the wetting of her neglected womanhood.

Olivia gracefully descended the winding staircase into the Sweet Rewards plantation house's wide foyer and through the crowd of admiring onlookers. She heard the sighs of women as they saw her in the exquisite dress, and she smiled, knowing her mother would be pleased. She walked directly to her parents and their guest. Olivia raised her head to reach her father's scarred cheek and plant a light kiss before bending to her mother's. She started to raise her hand to the tiara but decided against it. Magdalena, she was certain, had secured it.

"Olivia," her father said, taking her hand and passing it to the tall man next to him. "I would like to present you to Mr. James Devaroe of New Orleans and St. Louis."

Olivia curtseyed with her gloved hand, absorbing the heat from his through the cloth. "So very nice to make your acquaintance, Mr. Devaroe," Olivia said, holding his hand just a bit too tightly for convention but reluctant to break the connection.

"And I to make yours, Mademoiselle Thibodeaux." He brushed her fingers with his lips, and Olivia momentarily regretted the gloves.

Olivia yanked her hand back. "Mrs. Montgomery," she snapped. "It is Mrs. William Montgomery."

"Of course," he amended. "Pardon my ignorance. I meant you no disrespect, Mrs. Montgomery."

"Of course you didn't, James." Armand Thibodeaux slapped Devaroe's shoulder while he gave his daughter a disapproving glare. "Let's all go into the dining room and be seated. I believe the cooks have been working their fingers to the bones for this fine dinner."

James Devaroe offered Olivia his arm, and she reluctantly took it. They followed her parents into the dining room where Georgia and Magdalena had set the twelve-foot cypress table with the Thibodeaux family china, fine crystal and, gold-plated flatware upon bright white linen. Brass candelabras, gleaming like gold, sat every few places apart, giving a brilliant, glittering effect to the elegant table.

Her parents took their places at either end of the long table. Olivia found her place card sitting next to Devaroe's near the center while others found theirs. Some were seated at the main table with the hosts, while the hostess relegated others to smaller tables situated around the room. One of those was Simon Montrose, the arrogant son of a neighboring planta-tion owner and an ardent suitor for Olivia's hand for many years. Olivia could tell by his narrow-eyed stare that he felt slighted by this insult, and she smiled inwardly at his displeasure. Simon Montrose would have been her last choice as a husband, and her father knew it. They had rebuffed Montrose's of-fers for years, refusing to allow Sweet Rewards ever to fall into the hands of the Montrose family.

Simon's irritated glare at her father tempered Olivia's ire at James Devaroe, and she lifted her champagne glass to her slightly rouged lips and sipped. This vintage she found more to her liking than some, with a sweet rather than dry taste. She emptied her glass in one long swallow.

Armand Thibodeaux stood with his stemmed glass in hand when waiters in white waistcoats and black trousers made certain everyone had cham-pagne in their glasses. An impressive figure of a man, even with the hideous scar that marred and twisted the right side of his face, he raised his glass and tapped it with his fork. The room quieted.

"I would like to thank you all for coming tonight," he said in a clear, deep Creole-accented voice. "I would like us all to drink a toast to my lovely daughter, Olivia, and my dear friend James Devaroe of Devaroe Shipping and Cartage. Many of you know him, I am sure, and do business with his fine company." Thibodeaux raised his glass toward the couple and then drank, signaling the others at the tables to also begin enjoying the fine vintage before them.

At one of the satellite tables, a chair scraped across the polished marble floor, and someone cleared his throat. Everyone looked over to see Simon Montrose standing and looking pointedly toward Olivia and Devaroe, while his stoic white-haired father, Sterling Montrose, sat looking on with an aggravated frown. His glass sat on the table untouched. He only stood a few inches taller than Olivia's five-foot-six but was of a muscular build. He wore his stringy brown hair long to his shoulders and had a long whip-thin twisted mustache and pointed goatee.

"Monsieur Thibodeaux, I find it revolting that you would offer your lovely daughter to this pirating scum when I, a man of long-standing, local blood, unashamed of the spelling of my good French name, have made numerous offers of an honorable marriage and a joining of our two fine houses."

Olivia saw her father's and Devaroe's faces darken with Montrose's insults. She placed her gloved hand over James Devaroe's clenched one and gave her head a slight shake. He eased a little. Olivia saw the tension leave his shoulders, and his hand relaxed beneath hers.

"Simon," her father said, deliberately using the less formal first name of his offending guest, "while your offers have been sincerely received, my daughter has on regular occasion refused them. She is a grown woman and, I fear, has a mind of her own. She will take a husband again when she sees fit and not one minute before. It has ever been beyond my ability to change her mind on that accord."

"Perhaps that is true, Armand," Simon Montrose said with a doubtful smirk, "but I still cannot believe you would countenance this *nouveau riche* pretender to soil your fine bloodline. His parentage is that of pirates, for God's sake."

Olivia felt Devaroe tense again like a cat about to spring on its prey. She held tight to his hand, hoping to keep him from leaping over the table and attacking the odious Simon Montrose.

"Furthermore," Montrose continued to bait her father, "I always assumed you kept a tighter rein on the women of your family. If you told the girl to marry, she should, as an obedient daughter, feel it her familial duty to obey her father and wed the man of *his* choosing. She *is* obedient under your roof, is she not, Armand?"

Simon Montrose walked to the table directly across from Olivia, who stood to face him but kept a hand on Devaroe's shoulder to keep him in his seat. "Olivia Thibodeaux Montgomery," he said, holding out his own gloved hand over the table to her. "I again offer you my hand in marriage to unite two good Louisiana families and two prosperous plantations into one."

The tension in the air hung as heavy as the humidity on the hot June evening hung over the steamy bayou. "Simon Montrose, you officious little fool, I wouldn't have your hand in marriage if you were the last man of any bloodline in this mosquito-infested swamp," Olivia seethed. "Now, please sit back down like a good little boy and stop insulting my father and his guest or get out of our home so we can enjoy the rest of our evening." Several ladies in the room, including her mother, stood and clapped while Simon

Montrose, followed by his father Sterling, stormed from the dining room, slamming the door behind them as they exited the mansion.

Olivia took her seat along with the other ladies, several giggling at Montrose's humiliation. Armand Thibodeaux tapped his wine glass with a fork again and stood.

"Thank you, daughter, for ridding us of that buzzing mosquito," he said and smiled at Olivia with pride. "I told him she had a mind of her own." The room broke out in loud laughter. "Again, a toast to my lovely, mule-headed daughter, Olivia Thibodeaux Montgomery."

❧   3   ❧

"Mrs. Montgomery," James Devaroe said to her as he forked up a slice of succulent roast pork from his plate, "you certainly know how to put a man in his place."

"Does that bother you, Mr. Devaroe?" she asked him between bites of potatoes dripping with savory pork gravy. The mood in the room had become much lighter after Montrose's exit. The orchestra took up playing once more, and conversations buzzed all around them.

"*Au contraire,* I find a strong woman very intriguing," he said with a smile. "I suppose you have to be strong to survive out here in this wilderness."

Olivia's eyes darted around the lavish room, where the light sparkled off the crystal goblets, gold flatware, and expensive china, and she smiled. "I would hardly call Sweet Rewards a wilderness outpost, but managing any business builds one's character. I'm sure it's the same with your shipping line. Is it not?"

"I suppose it is," he agreed and sipped from his champagne glass. "I have four riverboats, twelve barges with tugs, and a whole fleet of cartage wagons with teams. Keeping track of it all can be quite un-nerving at times. I have managers in New Orleans and St. Louis, of course, but I still try to keep a tight rein on things."

Olivia admired his strength and his ability to contain his obvious anger during Montrose's rant. She also admired the fact that he had allowed her to take the lead in rebuffing Montrose. Some men would surely have felt belittled by that.

"Your father seems to have a pretty good handle on things here at Sweet Rewards."

"Everything except his mule-headed daughter," Olivia said and laughed. "Father has been trying to marry me off since William's death at Vicksburg. But I suppose you already knew that." Olivia finished her plate and dabbed her linen napkin at the corners of her mouth to make certain none of the brown gravy remained there.

"Your father," Devaroe said after emptying his champagne glass and setting it aside when the waiter offered a refill, "is a very astute businessman. He wants to make certain Sweet Rewards is in capable hands should his health fail him, or he suffer an acci-dent." Then he added, "The good Lord forbid," and crossed himself.

Armand Thibodeaux stood again at the head of the long table. "I believe we gentlemen will adjourn to my study for cigars while the ladies retreat to the parlor with my good wife before we have our dessert and coffee at the end of the hour. I believe Cook has prepared us a lovely orange marmalade cake."

To approving chatter, the two sexes moved to their respective domains, except Olivia and James Devaroe. He followed her through French doors onto a brick patio where candles made from the aromatic mosquito-repelling tansy plant were lit and sitting on round wrought-iron tables. The air wafted cool and damp from the earlier rain, and the tails of lightning bugs flickered over the manicured lawn beyond the short brick wall separating the two areas.

"It's a lovely evening," he told her as he took a seat upon the low wall, which would, undoubtedly, dampen the seat of his expensive trousers. He took no mind of it, and she caught him staring at her in the flickering glow of the candles.

Olivia luxuriated in the cool breeze left in the aftermath of the earlier storm. Now, with the clouds gone, stars twinkled in the black heavens above where only a sliver of moon hung to illuminate the night. Tree frogs squeaked in the nearby woods, and the musical calling of night birds replaced the stringed instruments of the orchestra inside.

"Yes," she replied and took a seat close to him. Olivia could feel the heat from his body and smelled his masculinity.

I've gone too damned long without a man between my legs.

The throbbing of her womanhood began again as she breathed in his aroma. The scents, a combination of Bay Rum shaving tonic, cigars, liquor, and man-sweat, dizzied her senses. The excitation more than she could bear, Olivia stood and stepped away from him. The tingling in her nipples attested to her arousal and added to her discomfort.

Devaroe followed her across the patio and laid his strong hot hands upon her bare shoulders between her diamond choker and the sleeves of her elegant dress. Although it was a bold, ungentlemanly action, Olivia found herself leaning back into his embrace, allowing the heat of his touch to flow through her very being and melting into him like the wax of the candles around her.

Olivia felt his lips brush the top of her left ear,

and the heat of his breath there released a hot flow of passion between her thighs. She wanted more than anything to turn around and taste his mouth. She wanted to feel those lips upon hers, and she wanted him to feel hers. Goose flesh broke out upon her arms, and the tiny hairs rose in anticipation of another touch.

Devaroe turned her around and brushed her cheek with those hot full lips, trying to get to her mouth, but she pulled away. She wanted his touch more than anything she'd wanted in a long while, but she resisted for convention's sake.

"This is unseemly, Mr. Devaroe," she said, backing reluctantly away. "We don't know one another nearly well enough to be spooning on my father's patio."

"Pardon my misassumptions, Mrs. Montgomery," he told her and walked stiff-backed past her and into the house.

Misassumptions? Does he think I lured him out here to do illicit things in the dark? The throbbing in her groin persisted. *Did I?*

A mosquito buzzed around her ear, and she slapped at it. She could still feel his hot breath on that ear, and the thought of it only caused her throbbing discomfort to intensify. Olivia had not felt this way around a man in years. Did it mean her love for William had waned away? Could that possibly be?

"Livvy, what you doin' out here in the dark alone?" Olivia jerked her head up with a start at the sound of Magdalena's voice. "You better be comin' in," she told her, and Olivia noted Magdalena wore a serving maid's uniform. "We gonna start servin' dessert in a few minutes. Why that riverboat man go stormin' through the house the way he did? You say somethin' to make him mad already? Daddy ain't going to like that none if you did."

"I just wouldn't kiss him," Olivia sighed.

"Lord have mercy, girl, why not? That man looks sweet as honey on cornbread," she giggled, "and hot cornbread at that."

"Magda, I am going to swat you if you don't stop being crude." Olivia stormed past her half-sister, who stood giggling as she passed, and returned to her seat in the dining room. All the ladies sat in their respective seats, waiting for the men to return. Her mother gave her a hopeful smile and arched an eyebrow as if in question. Olivia returned the smile but did not know or care what it conveyed.

Devaroe returned to his seat next to her, and she could smell the strong scent of tobacco and brandy on him. He had joined her father and the others in the study for a smoke and a drink. His nearness brought about another flush to her face, and when she glanced at her mother, she knew Marie Thibodeaux saw it from the satisfied grin on her pale, thin face. Olivia suspected her mother already had the guest list and wedding invitations in mind as she sat there smirking at her red-faced daughter.

After dessert and coffee in the dining room, the guests chatted and mingled for another hour before beginning to filter out of the mansion. Only James Devaroe remained. He would be ensconced in the guest suite just down the hall from Olivia's room. The thought of him sleeping so near brought up her color again, and she poured another glass of champagne in an effort to quell it.

A butler escorted Devaroe to his room, and Olivia bid her parents a good night soon after.

"Thank you for a lovely party, Father," she said and kissed his scarred cheek.

"What do you think of him, Livvy? Do you like him, or should I send a note of capitulation to Simon?"

Olivia rolled her eyes and slapped her father on the shoulder. "That's up to you, Daddy. I am ever your obedient daughter."

"That will be a cold day in Hell," her father said and laughed. "I'm proud of you, girl, for putting that officious fool, Simon Montrose, in his place, though. You are of true Thibodeaux blood."

"Even if I'm just a lowly female Thibodeaux?" Olivia kissed her mother and walked to the stairs with the orchid silk swishing about her legs as she stepped.

"You looked beautiful tonight, *ma Cherie*," her mother called after her.

"*Bonsoir, ma mere.* We will talk about this in the morning. I'm exhausted."

In her room, Olivia stripped out of the lovely dress. With Magdalena's help loosening the cords of her corset, she finished undressing and took down her hair.

"So, Miss Livvy," Magdalena teased, "how do you like that rich riverboat man? Did Daddy finally find you, someone you'd consider fit to marry?" She pulled out the final pin, and Olivia's hair tumbled down like midnight rivers to fall below her shoulders and cover her firm white breasts. Just thinking about James Devaroe's hot, strong hands on her bare shoulders brought her nipples to attention once more and a throbbing between her thighs.

"He is, indeed, an interesting man." She ran her fingers through her hair and scratched her scalp with her nails. The relief at having her hair released from the confining, tight bun paled against the relief of being able to breathe again with the escape from the confining corset.

"Interesting and handsome." Magdalena giggled. "Mammy told me to dress nice and gave me some silk stockings and fancy garters to wear to his bed tonight. I am supposed to entertain the riverboat man in his room."

"What?" Olivia stood and stormed out the door of her room. First, she intended to speak with her father about this ridiculous house-slave bullshit but changed her mind and marched down the hall to the guest room. She found herself in front of the door and resolutely knocked.

"Come in, my dear," she heard him call from inside the room and pushed open the heavy oak door. James Devaroe lay naked on the bed, stroking his large, erect penis. When he realized who stood there, he scrambled to cover himself with the quilt folded at the foot of the bed.

"My sister will not be joining you in your bed tonight, Mr. Devaroe, or any other," Olivia growled.

"Your sister?" Confusion contorted his handsome face, and he continued to pull at the quilt that lay over his erection and his bared loins. "I have no idea what you are talking about, Mrs. Montgomery. Your father said he was sending up a house girl to take care of this condition you left me in." He pulled at the quilt over his erection. "What do you mean about a sister?"

"That house girl just happens to be my father's daughter, too. She is my half-sister and my maid." Olivia turned when she realized he gaped at her wide-eyed. Wearing only her flimsy summer dressing gown, she realized it now hung open down the front, exposing her naked breasts, belly, groin, and legs.

"You came in her place then?" He smirked, not

taking his eyes off her body. "How very gallant of you, Mrs. Montgomery." He pulled the quilt from his body to reveal his erection to her. Olivia, to her shame, imagined it sliding between her legs or lying throbbing against her belly, and her nipples stiffened again along with the wetting of her throbbing groin. In her mind, she could feel his tongue brushing over those nipples and his teeth grazing them.

She pulled her dressing gown together. "I'm afraid you are going to have to service yourself tonight, Mr. Devaroe." Olivia turned red-faced and stormed from his room. This man infuriated her. He intrigued her, but he also infuriated her.

Storming back into her room with her hair hanging loose about her head and her gown falling open again, Magdalena met her laughing in snorting fits. "You went down to that riverboat man's room and made a damned fool of yourself, didn't you, Livvy Montgomery? You are besotted with that man. Just admit it."

"I may be interested, but that doesn't mean I'm going to let him use you the same way he might use a paid woman in a cat house," Olivia told her sister. "And I'm going to speak with my father about this. You are no longer a slave in this house, and he can't pass you around at his discretion. You are a free woman who can decide for herself who she does and does not want to bed with."

"Maybe I *wanted* to bed with that rich riverboat man," Magdalena teased her. "You aren't the only one who hasn't bedded with a handsome man in a good long while."

"That may be, little sister, but I'm laying claim to this one," Olivia said and giggled.

❧ 4 ☙

The morning after the party at Sweet Rewards dawned sunny and hot. While eating their breakfast on Olivia's veranda, she and Magdalena watched James Devaroe walk off across the grounds.

"Where you think he's goin'? Magdalena asked as she poured honey into her tea.

"Probably going out to inspect his prospective holdings," Olivia sneered and took a bite of her buttered croissant. She watched the man cross the green lawn and slip down a path through the woods surrounding the property that led toward the swampy bayou area around the cane fields.

"Why don't we take a walk today?" Olivia sipped her tea as she watched Devaroe disappear into the brush and palmetto at the edge of the lawn.

Magdalena followed Olivia's eyes and smiled. "It's a bit warm for a walk, Livvy, but if you insist."

They finished their meal, dressed, and left the house. Magdalena took the lead and headed across the lawn in the same direction they had seen Devaroe go. "I assume this is the direction you wanted to stroll this mornin'."

Down the path, shaded by the overhanging

branches of oaks and cypresses, thick with Spanish Moss spilling over them, they walked until they heard splashing. Olivia pulled Magdalena behind the thick trunk of a giant cypress and looked around to see James Devaroe swimming in one of the shallow ponds on the property.

"That riverboat man might be rich," Magdalena snorted, "but he's plenty stupid goin' swimmin' out here in this swamp. He's gonna be gator bait if he don't get out of that pond."

As if hearing her, James Devaroe pulled himself up on the narrow dock built out into the water by the plantation's fishermen. He wasn't wearing a stitch. His tall, tanned body glistened with water as he stretched out his lean, hard-muscled limbs on the boards. He balled his clothes up and tucked them under his head. As they watched, his hand moved down over his tight, flat stomach to his groin and began fondling his penis into a massive erection.

"Hellfire," Magdalena said and giggled, "this might be an interesting walk after all."

Olivia smiled at her sister and peeked back around the big tree. Devaroe busied himself, stroking his cock with his right hand, running it first down to its base and then back up over the purplish bulb at the top. He repeated the action and watching the act brought a tingling throb once more to Olivia's groin. She shivered as she imagined that beautiful thing slamming into her, and she moaned with the thought.

"I hear that, sister," Magdalena concurred. "I wouldn't mind me a little of that slidin' into my black cunny. Maybe we could share him. It sure looks like he got more than enough for two."

Olivia ignored the mosquitos flitting around her sweaty head and watched the naked figure on the dock pleasuring himself. She imagined ripping off her skirts, running to him, and straddling that beautiful, stiff cock. She closed her eyes, swallowed hard, and imagined how it would feel lowering her body onto the hard staff, rising from between his well-defined thighs, and riding it until she exploded with those exquisite waves of pleasure between her thighs.

When she opened them again, she saw him massaging his large, dark ballocks with his left hand before arching his back up off the old gray boards as his fisted hand slid over his cock faster, and he groaned loudly with the explosive shot of thick white fluid that squirted up and onto his hard, tanned belly. She watched and wished she had been the one eliciting and receiving that thick milky deposit.

"Yes, I most certainly think he's got plenty for two, Livvy," Magdalena sighed. "I ain't never seen a man pleasure himself like that before. Have you?"

"No," Olivia admitted, absently brushing a mosquito away from her head and trying to ignore the annoying throbbing between her thighs.

Look at me, skulking behind a tree, spying on a man in his most private moment. What have I become? Mother is right. Seven years is simply too long to have kept me from a man. Perhaps I should visit the guest room tonight and give James Devaroe a try. Maybe if he thinks I'm a disrespectable wanton woman, he'll go away and forget about this marriage nonsense.

"Be quiet, Magda. I don't want him to hear us. He'll think we're spying on him."

"But we *are* spying on him and that beautiful cock of his," she whispered with a giggle. "I'd sure like me some of that pretty white cock between my legs. How 'bout you, Livvy?"

"I've been thinking the same thing, Magda." She glanced back to the dock where Devaroe lay, seemingly asleep with one muscular arm across his face and the other hand still clenching his ballocks. "It has been too damned long."

Olivia pulled Magdalena away from the tree and back up the path toward the house.

"Daddy's gonna be happy to hear that."

Remembering the sight of Devaroe naked in his bed and picturing herself naked and crawling in with him, she doubted her father would appreciate her plans for the night. Olivia shushed Magdalena again and continued to pull her up the path until they found themselves on the green lawn adjacent to the house's back patio, where her mother lounged in the shade, fanning away mosquitos and stirring a breeze.

Marie Thibodeaux waved when she saw them and motioned them over to join her. Olivia released her hold on Magdalena's arm and joined her mother in the cooler shade.

"Whatever have you girls been doing out there in the brush?" She fanned with more vigor and picked up a heavy glass tumbler of sweet tea. "Olivia, make certain you check yourself for ticks. The dogs have been absolutely infested with them this summer, and I don't want you coming down with tick fever." She sipped her tea as Olivia joined her, and Magdalena went into the house. "I heard the LaRue boy died of it last week. I don't know how I am going to abide another funeral of a child."

"Mother, they had his funeral mass the next day. It's too hot to keep a body for more than a day after death during this heat."

"Yes, of course, they did, *Cherie.* It has my mind all in a jumble. Now tell me," her mother asked, fanning away another annoying mosquito, "what did you really think of our Mr. Devaroe?"

Olivia's mind flashed back to the scene she had just witnessed on the dock, and she felt the heat flushing her cheeks. Like the touch of a ghostly lover, the breeze caressed the damp, bare skin of her arms. Just the thought of the man's naked form made her entire body sensitive, and her nipples hardened and ached for the touch of his lips upon them.

"He is quite a magnificent specimen," she blurted before thinking about to whom she spoke.

"Yes, he is," Marie replied and smiled with satisfaction at her daughter. "Your father will be pleased to hear you are not completely dismissing him out of hand."

"Mother, I've only just met the man. Don't go putting us into a marriage bed quite yet." Olivia picked up her mother's glass of tea and took a sip, somewhat surprised to taste more than just tea in the sweet concoction. She replaced the glass hastily, hoping her mother hadn't seen her take the drink. Since her *riding accident* the year before, requiring her use of the cane to walk, Marie was known to partake of the liquor cabinet's contents more than just occasionally.

Olivia and everyone residing in the Sweet Rewards plantation house knew Marie had not ridden in years. Her *accident* had occurred in her bedroom at the hands of her drunken husband while on one of his lecherous binges when he beat and abused her, cracking her pelvis and keeping her in her bed for weeks afterward. Such had been the marriage bed of Marie and Armand Thibodeaux for as long as Olivia could recall. According to Magdalena, he used her mother, Georgia, in much the same fashion.

Perhaps that was one of the reasons Olivia had loved William so. He had been a sweet and gentle lover, always attentive to her needs and desires before his own. She was thinking of her sweet, gentle William when James Devaroe came walking onto the lawn from the woods. Marie looked at her daughter and raised an enquiring eyebrow.

"Good afternoon, ladies," he greeted them, wiping sweat from his forehead with a silk handkerchief. "This is a lovely, shaded space." He pulled up the legs of his wrinkled trousers and sat in one of the cushioned wrought-iron chairs.

Marie rose, picked up her glass, and hobbled back toward the door to the house. "I need a refill," she told them. Devaroe jumped out of his seat to open the door for her. "Thank you, James. I will have Georgia bring you both a glass." Marie disappeared into the house, leaving Olivia alone with Devaroe on the shady patio.

He took the liberty of sitting in the chair at the small round table next to her. Olivia picked up her mother's discarded silk fan and began waving it in front of her face.

"Did you enjoy your walk, Mrs. Montgomery?" he asked with a sly smile.

"Excuse me?" Olivia asked and felt her cheeks flushing once more.

Did he know we were there watching him? Was he putting on a show for us?

"You and your sister would not make very good scouts, I'm afraid." He chuckled. "You made enough noise to scare up every rabbit and small bird for a mile, and that perfume you wear is quite distinctive. Orange blossom, I believe?"

"You knew we were there, and you still ..." Her fan moved even faster, and her head told her to stand while her throbbing loins told her to stay put.

"That scent brings something out in me that I can't seem to control. Did you and your sister enjoy the show?"

Olivia took a deep breath and smiled. "Indeed

we did, Mr. Devaroe. And as my Mother was telling me earlier, you should make certain to check yourself for ticks. They are bad this year." She laid the fan down and stood. "You should also check yourself for leeches. That little pond is positively full of them."

Devaroe reached out and took her free hand, pulling her close. "Perhaps you'd like to come to my room tonight and make the inspection yourself." From her skirt, he picked off a tiny brown thing, holding it so she could see its tiny wiggling legs. "You see, I just saved you from one. Now it's your duty to return the favor."

His strong hand holding hers ignited one fire in her, but his arrogant attitude ignited another. "You presume too much, Mr. Devaroe," she said, jerking her hand from his.

He stood, took her arm, and raised it until he had her wrist under his nose. He inhaled deeply over the spot where she applied her neroli oil, made from the blossoms of bitter oranges.

"I told you that scent makes me lose all control." He inhaled again before dropping her arm. "It's absolutely enchanting," he told her with a grin, "just like the beautiful woman who wears it."

They were interrupted by Magdalena coming through the door with a pitcher of tea and two glasses. "I have y'all's tea, Miss Livvy." She set the tray on the table, poured tea in the two glasses, and gave Olivia a little wink and a smile. "Enjoy," she told them and returned with some haste to the large house.

"That's your sister?" Devaroe asked as he picked up one of the tumblers to hand to her. "I don't see the resemblance."

"Luckily, we both look like our respective mothers and not our father, although Father was

considered a very handsome man before his unfortunate scarring."

Devaroe took her head by the chin and turned it
from side to side, examining her face. "I think you
must be correct, but with Armand's scar, it's hard to
tell. You do have your mother's fine features, though.
They remind me of those on the marble statues of
Greek goddesses, very delicate and perfectly propor-
tioned. I saw some at the museums in Paris."

"You have visited Paris?" she asked with awed
enthusiasm.

"Yes, I went to school there in my youth and
stayed until just before the War. I came home when
there was a certainty of a conflict. My father required my help with the business."

"The pirating business?" she asked, referring to
Montrose's insults of the night before.

"Privateers," he corrected. "My father had ships
that ran the Union blockade of New Orleans. We've
had ships doing business with the Islands for decades,
though."

"Why do you not spell your name in the French
fashion then?"

"When my ancestors came to Louisiana from
Canada in the last century, they'd already changed
the spelling. Something to do with their business
dealings with the British back then, I believe." He
took a long drink of his tea. "My mother said it is
spelled this way in the family Bible, so it's the way it
is written on the baptismal and marriage records. I
suppose I could go to a magistrate and have the
spelling changed, but it would cause all sorts of problems with business contracts and the like."

Olivia nodded. "I can see where that could be a
problem. Father has a whole floor of lawyers doing
his business in New Orleans. I can just imagine the

ruckus it would raise if he went in and told him he wanted to change our name's spelling. It would take clerks months to go through all the paperwork."

"And you only have the sugar plantation," he told her with a chuckle as he stretched his long, lean body and yawned. "I have the boats and barges on the rivers, the schooners that run to the Islands, and the cartage division. I have contracts with hundreds of different businesses from Jamaica to Minneapolis."

He watched her face, and Olivia thought he must be looking for signs of her being impressed with his extensive holdings. She smiled and watched his eyes as he continued. "I just commissioned a shipbuilder in San Francisco to build me three frigates to start sailing into the South Seas and to China. Devaroe shipping will be an international concern very soon."

"That is very impressive, Mr. Devaroe. You have been to San Francisco?" The thought of that exotic city enthralled her. Olivia only dreamed of escaping from the Louisiana swamp. She and her family had visited Martinique once on a business trip, but that was as far away from Sweet Rewards as Olivia had ever been. Before marrying William, she had attended finishing school in New Orleans and dreamed of visiting Paris someday like all the other girls. William had promised to take her to Virginia to meet his family and visit their horse farm, but the war had put an end to that.

"I have not yet had the pleasure," he replied. "My business there was done over the telegraph and through intermediaries. When the ships are complete, I plan to be there to watch them set sail," he said and took her hand. "I am hoping to have a wife to be there with me to launch their maiden voyages."

They dined privately that evening, using the common china and the silver flatware. They ate spicy shrimp and rice with biscuits and butter. A delicate white wine accompanied the meal, and they chatted amiably over their food. Olivia sat close to Devaroe at the table, the heat from his body radiating into her from his nearness. She could smell his Bay Rum over the spices of the dinner, and it aroused her beyond belief. It was all she could do to keep from reaching for him under the table, but she managed to control herself and kept her hand respectably in her lap.

"So, James," Armand Thibodeaux said between bites, "my daughter tells me you are stepping up your shipping empire and moving into the Orient."

"Yes, that seems to be where the future of trade is coming from, and the Celestials pay huge sums for transport here to the States."

"Fools," Olivia sighed. "They pay huge sums to come to this country to be taken advantage of and treated no better than slaves when they get here by unscrupulous mine owners and the railroads."

"Perhaps you can bring some of them down here

to Louisiana, James," her father said and laughed. "I understand most of them are accustomed to our climate and understand the farming of rice. We could use that good cheap labor here."

"Father, you already have a plantation filled with Negro indentures who work for almost nothing."

"Child, just leave the matters of business to the men. You have no concept of what it takes to sustain a profitable business."

"Father, I've been shadowing your footsteps here on Sweet Rewards since I could walk." Olivia stabbed a shrimp in her shallow bowl with such vigor that it splashed sauce out onto the tablecloth. "I understand the economics of this business better than you think. I may just be a silly, weak-minded female who you consider nothing but a broodmare for your heir to Sweet Rewards, but I guarantee you that if you dropped dead tomorrow, I could step in and run this plantation just as well."

"Olivia, *ma Cherie*," her mother interrupted, "let's not air our laundry in front of our guest."

"*Ma mere*, y'all intend this man to be my husband. Shouldn't he become accustomed to our laundry?"

"Olivia Marie," her father stormed, pounding a fist on the table. "Do not be insolent." He turned to James, his face red with anger and embarrassment, "Please excuse my daughter, James. I'm afraid I've indulged her overmuch throughout her life. She has not learned any respect. Perhaps *you* will be able to teach her some."

"So, have you settled upon terms for my breeding services to Mr. Devaroe, Father?" Olivia stormed and darted her eyes between her father and Devaroe. "What kind of price did you get for my hand, Daddy, free shipping for a lifetime?" She stood, knocking her chair over, and turned to leave the room.

"Olivia, my dear." James Devaroe grabbed her hand before she could escape from the table and out of the room. "I want you for my wife. I'll not deny that, but if you choose to reject me, I can respect that. You're not a bale of cotton to be bartered over in the marketplace." He dropped her hand, but she did not leave.

Instead, she righted the chair and sat. "So, have you agreed-upon terms?" she asked without looking at any of them. The strong grasp of Devaroe's hand on her skin brought back the memories of the morning, and desire rose in her like the boiling of water in a pot.

Her father cleared his throat. "Yes, we have agreed upon a bride price, and all you have to do is agree upon a date for the wedding."

"So how much did he squeeze you for?" Olivia asked Devaroe as she watched her parents squirm in their chairs. "I'm sure he didn't let me go cheap even though I'm *used* goods and have never conceived a child to prove my worth as a breeder."

"No, he certainly did not," Devaroe laughed. "I had to promise him ten years of shipping contracts for the plantation and to reduce my business contracting with the other plantations he competes with."

"Well, after we have wed, you can forgo that silliness." Olivia glared at her glowering father. "You cannot ignore business opportunities for something you already possess, and if you ignore business opportunities, you will deny me the funds I'll need for travel to places like Paris and San Francisco."

"Nonsense, daughter," her father said, "you'll be staying right here on Sweet Rewards unless you're traveling with your husband."

"I will travel wherever I please. This plantation

will be the death of me if I don't get away for a while. I can't very well conceive an heir to this palace in the swamp if I'm locked up here, and my husband is off in San Francisco or St. Louis," Olivia said calmly as she wiped her mouth and stood again. "Mother, you can choose a date." She scowled at her father. "Getting away from here can't be soon enough." She turned and left the room this time, clacking her wooden heels on the marble floor as she walked.

❧

James Devaroe watched her storm off and listened to her shoes as she mounted the stairs. He glanced at Armand's face and smiled to himself. Even if he didn't appreciate her for more than a female to carry his heir for this plantation, the man had raised an amazing daughter.

I think this is a woman with whom I could spend the rest of my life. Armand may be correct, and she needs a bit of taming, the way a prize mare needs to be tamed by its new master, but I see that as a challenge I'm willing to accept.

Armand cleared his throat and lifted his glass. "Shall we toast then to the nuptials of the happy couple?"

Marie lifted her glass. "Has the contract been signed then?" she asked hesitantly.

"It has," Armand said in reply, "and I'd suggest you go to her room tonight, James, and consummate the contract now before my headstrong daughter takes it into her fool mind to disobey me."

"Armand," Marie gasped, "they have not been wed by a priest yet."

Armand Thibodeaux glared at his wife across the long table. "I spoke to a priest some time ago about this, Marie, and he told me that in the eyes of the church, once the betrothal has been made and I agree to the terms of a marriage contract, and a ring has been offered and accepted, the couple may consummate the bond." He grinned. "The good Father said it was a way to make certain the prospective bride does not then try to renege in some way. Once consummated, they are as good as married in the eyes of the Church."

Marie's eyes went wide. "But no ring was offered or accepted," she said.

Devaroe took a pearl ring from his pocket and showed it to Olivia's mother. "I swear she will wear this ring before I consummate this marriage contract, Madam Thibodeaux. I would do nothing to shame you or my intended bride in your home."

❧

Olivia kicked her shoes off in her room, sending one clattering into the wall beneath the window.

I am escaping this God-awful swamp if it is the last thing I ever do. I should have stayed in the townhouse in New Orleans after the Yankees killed my William. Yankees and war be damned. If I'd died, at least I'd be with William, even if it meant being entombed here forever on Sweet Rewards. I'd be dead rather than dying a lingering death as I am now.

Olivia unbuttoned her dress and let it fall to the floor. She wanted to open the French doors in the hopes of a breeze, but it would mean allowing hordes of mosquitos into her room for the night. Olivia poured water at the washbasin, dipped a cloth, and wiped down her sweaty brow, neck, and bosoms. She slipped out of her camisole and dropped her bloomers, wiping the cool rag over her naked body. Unable to get comfortable, Olivia dropped onto the bed and stared at the doors to the veranda. Maybe if she lit some of the tansy candles, it would dissuade the little buzzing beasts so she could get some air. Then again, the heat from the candles would only make things worse.

Olivia stood again, naked before the washbasin, cloth in hand, when she heard the door from the hall open. She turned, expecting to see either Magdalena or her mother there, but her mouth fell open in shock to see James Devaroe standing there, turning the key to lock the door behind him.

Grabbing up her dressing gown, Olivia tried to cover herself. In two strides, Devaroe stood in front of her. He tugged the gown away and tossed it on the floor. Unbuttoning his silk shirt one silver button at a time, he held her gaze. She watched the thick black hair on his broad, tanned chest begin to peek through the gap in the white silk. Olivia grabbed his black vest and pushed it off his shoulders like a brazen woman.

Devaroe wrapped his arms around her white body, glistening with sweat from her arousal as well as the sticky Louisiana heat.

"You sparkle like the icy snow on the banks of the Mississippi in Minnesota, but you are far from cold, Mrs. Montgomery." She felt his hands running down her back to settle upon the cheeks of her derriere. He pulled her into his hot body and buried his face into the hair on the top of her head. His hot breath there sent shivers of excitement down her spine and ignited a fire in her groin.

Olivia let the excitement of the moment carry her away and lifted her face to meet his. She allowed his hot, soft lips to take her mouth and jumped back a little when a spark like lightning in the air ignited as their lips touched for that first time. He must have experienced it too and smiled down at her, baring his glistening white teeth.

"We are betrothed now, Mrs. Montgomery. It is allowed by the Church for us to couple as husband and wife without sin. Your parents have given their consent." Devaroe reached into his trouser pocket and brought out a gold ring set with a pearl resting between two bright yellow diamonds. He took her left hand in his and slipped the ring onto her finger. "This ring has been worn by the matriarchs of the Devaroe family since well before they sailed to Canada over two hundred years ago. I declare us betrothed and claim you as my own, Olivia Marie Thibodeaux Montgomery if you have me."

Olivia met his lips again and melted with the heat of his chest on her erect, aching nipples. She brushed his lips and breathed, "Yes, James Devaroe, I will take you as my husband."

Devaroe pulled her naked body closer and kissed her with a deep passion Olivia had not experienced in years. His tongue, which he'd snaked between her wanton lips, tasted like liquor and tobacco, but she didn't care. She slid her arms around him inside his unbuttoned shirt, returning his embrace.

Olivia shivered with excitement as his hands ran up and down her back and squeezed the firm cheeks of her behind. Using her fingernails, she scratched his back not with eagerness but with languishing and gentle teasing. He shivered under her touch, and goose flesh erupted over his body as he turned her toward the bed. Bending a little at the knee, he lifted her onto the mattress and laid her, so her head rested upon the white chenille-covered pillows. Devaroe shed his shirt, unbuckled his belt, and let his trousers fall to the floor around his bare feet.

Olivia looked at his hard, toned body with muscles rippling in his arms and thighs and smiled in anticipation of becoming one with it. The thick, coarse black hair on his chest narrowed below his hard nipples but continued in a line over his rippling belly to connect with that around his erect penis and dark brown ballocks. She reached out and caressed the testicles, which elicited a groan of pleasure from the man, who joined her on the bed, bending over her to kiss one of her hard nipples. That brought about a pleasurable groan from her, and her body quivered.

Olivia moved her hand up from the hanging sack to encircle the erect shaft above it; the girth was such that her fingers barely met her thumb. Devaroe moved closer to her so she could get a good hold and reached a hand down to knead her breasts, pinching her nipples. Those pinches made her moan with delight as her womanhood moistened, awaiting his entry. He ran his hand from her breast down over her flat belly to probe the throbbing wetness between her thighs, which brought more pleasurable moans from deep in her chest.

Devaroe took those moans as a cue and moved down to straddle her thighs and thrust himself deep into her. After going seven years without a man, she must have been tight. He groaned as if in pain, but she watched him smiling and knew it to be a pleasurable pain.

"You are like a virgin, *ma Cherie*," he panted as he continued to thrust into her, causing Olivia to pant as well. She ran her hands over his taut thighs and pulled him into her. He bent and kissed her neck, sometimes sucking hard at her tender flesh or nipping it with his teeth. He reached under her backside, dug his fingers into her, and pulled her body up to meet his, causing some pain to her. She groaned and flinched, but he gripped her harder.

Olivia tried to wiggle free, but the movement appeared to intensify his pleasure, and he dug his nails into her as if trying to get her to do it some more. She did, and he soon groaned out his release and fell on top of her, just short of her release, which frustrated Olivia. William had always held his until he was certain she had achieved her pleasure.

"Olivia, my dear, that was outstanding." He rolled off her and gave her thigh a hard slap, causing her to flinch. Her little jerk excited him, and soon he licked her breasts again. Then he rolled her over onto her stomach and began massaging her backside. Devaroe probed her cunny, wet with his fluid, and brought some of it up to massage between the cheeks until he probed the other cavity there, inserting first one finger, then, to her dismay, another.

"Didn't your last husband ever temper his sword in this?" he asked as she flinched when he shoved two fingers into her anus, eliciting a yelp of pain and displeasure from her, which again seemed to excite him. He wet himself inside her cunny, then brought his hard penis up and used it to massage her anus.

"Did he?" he demanded as he shoved into her backside with his hard, thick manhood.

"No!" She yelped with pain and tried to crawl away from beneath his weight. That scream excited him more, and Devaroe pushed into her completely. Olivia could feel his ballocks slamming against the cheeks of her backside as he thrust in and out of her, causing unbearable pain, but each time she winced or yelped with the pain, he got more excited and used her with more force.

"Let the pain amplify your pleasure, my dear," he whispered into her ear. "Here, let me help." Olivia felt his hand slide beneath her belly and down between her legs. He found the throbbing knot there and began to massage it in time with the thrusts into her backside. To her surprise, the combination of the pain in her anus and the pleasure of his massaging brought about an astounding release, and Olivia found herself meeting his thrusts until her groin exploded with waves of intense, throbbing pleasure.

"Oh, my god," she moaned as her body stiffened, and she rode the throbbing bursts of pleasure in her groin.

Her excitement brought about his release, and he shoved into her hard and groaned before rolling off her, panting and sweaty.

Devaroe turned to look at her and brought his hand up to brush a finger across her lips. "Is that virgin too?" He chuckled when he saw the horror in her eyes. "Don't worry, *Cherie*, I will be gentle with it."

Olivia could feel his fluids oozing from her and rolled off the bed. She wet the washcloth and wiped him from between her legs and butt cheeks. When she brought the cloth back to the basin, blood spotted it. Horrified, Olivia rinsed the cloth and wiped again. This time the cloth came away with more semen than blood from the tender orifice, which relaxed her.

"How is it that soldier-boy husband of yours never broke you in properly? You have three doorways to pleasure, and he only ever took the one?" he asked her, watching her clean up and fondling himself into a semi-erection.

Olivia glared down at the man she'd just agreed to marry and frowned. "I will not speak to you about what William and I did in our marriage bed. It is none of your business."

"I beg to differ," he said with a scowl, "but I will not speak of him again if that is what you wish."

"It is," Olivia said as she bent and retrieved his clothes from the floor. She pitched them to him on the bed. "You should leave now and return to *your* room." She picked up her dressing gown, covered her naked body, went to the French doors, and opened them. The cooler night air washed over her sweaty body as she walked out onto the veranda. At the railing, Olivia looked up at the night sky, sparkling with stars and a sliver of a moon.

William would never have used me like that. It would have gone against his very nature to inflict pain on me or to take his pleasure before I had mine. This relationship is a mistake. I can't spend my life with a man like this. He is just like Father, and I refuse to become a simpering victim like Mother.

Olivia glanced back into her room to see Devaroe sitting on the edge of the bed, tying his shoes. She walked back into the room, slid the pearl ring from her finger, and handed it to him. He looked up at her in dismay, furrowing his brow and opening his mouth to speak.

Olivia did not wait to hear what he had to say. She dropped the ring into his lap, went back through the French-doors, and closed them behind her. When Olivia peeked back into the room, she saw Devaroe dressed and bent over her writing desk. Shaken by the ordeal she had just endured in her bed, Olivia pulled the soft cotton dressing gown tight around her abused body, not against a chill in the night air but rather one running through her very being.

The stars sparkled brightly in the sky over mist-covered grounds Sweet Rewards, but Olivia heard distant thunder. With the feeling of a dark foreboding, she tread lithe as a cat over the boards of the veranda to peek again into her room. Finding it empty, Olivia opened the doors and entered. She ran a hand over her scalp to feel tender spots where Devaroe had pulled her hair. She did not remember him doing that, but he must have because when her hand came away, strands of tangled black hair came with it. Olivia let the hair fall to the floor, closed her eyes, and allowed tears of rage, pain, and disgust to slip down her cheeks.

Fearing his return, she went to the door to the hall and locked it. To reinforce the lock, she took the chair from her desk and propped it under the knob so the door, if unlocked somehow, could not be pushed open. Finally feeling safely barricaded in her private fortress, Olivia returned to her bed. The white chenille spread had blood spots on it, and she immediately went to the basin to get the wet cloth to try and clean it away.

She then saw a piece of her private stationery writing in a neat flowery script upon her pillow. On the sheath of paper lay the pearl ring. Olivia hesitated to pick up the paper, but she finally did, sliding it off her pillow, so the ring remained.

My Dearest Wife, Olivia,

You may choose to wear the ring or not. It is of no great care to me. But make no mistake; we are now, in the eyes of God, The Church, and any parish magistrates you may wish to approach, man and wife. I have a binding marriage contract with your Father, who accompanied me tonight to your room to hear the consummation of our union through the door. You accepted my proposal and my ring, and then you accepted me into your bed and your body. We are, by law, husband and wife now. The public ceremony is simply a formality that we can forego if you wish, but I believe it would comfort your mother some to have the ritual with a priest, dress, cake, and candles. Your

father and I will be very happy if you have conceived
a son tonight, but there will be many more nights here
for us to accomplish that. You make a most pleasing
bedmate.
    Your Husband, James Eduard Devaroe

Olivia read the words on the page several times, allowing their meaning to solidify in her brain. Then she took it to the lamp, set it to the flame, and watched it catch. Before the crimson light reached her fingers, Olivia dropped the paper, more black ash than not, into the water of her basin and watched it float and fizzle out in the liquid stained pink with her blood.

❧ 6 ❧

Olivia woke to frantic pounding on her door and, for a moment, feared Devaroe had returned. Then she heard her mother's panicked voice from the hall.

"Olivia, *ma Cherie*, are you ill? It is almost noon, and we have not seen you all morning. Let me in," Marie Thibodeaux pled in a frail voice, still rapping on the door.

"In a moment, *ma mere*." Olivia rolled over and felt pain shoot through the lower half of her body. The cheeks of her backside ached when she put pressure on them, and Olivia could tell James Devaroe had bruised them. She grabbed up her dressing gown and wrapped it around her as she stumbled to the door and removed the chair, securing her privacy.

As soon as Olivia turned the brass key in the lock, her mother burst through the door, supported by her silver-handled cane. "Are you ill, *ma petite?* You never sleep this late."

"I am fine, Mother. I simply did not sleep well last night." Olivia went to her bed and sat gingerly on the edge. Her mother joined her and took her hands and studied the left one as if searching for something. Olivia glanced at her side table, and her eyes fell upon Devaroe's ring. It still lay there where she'd dropped it before burying her head into her pillows in the early morning hours, sometime just before dawn.

"Your father and Mr. Devaroe told me you had accepted his ring and consummated your betrothal last evening." Olivia saw Marie eying William's picture lying face down on the table and her daughter's red and swollen eyes. "Are you not happy, daughter? Your William would want you to be happy, would he not?" Marie looked desperate, her hands shaking as she held her daughter's. She smiled then, trying to lighten the mood. "I have spoken with Georgia, and we will begin preparations for the wedding ceremony to be held here in the garden. We can take a carriage into New Orleans to have you fitted for a dress later this week." Marie continued to ramble on about invitations, flowers, and guest lists, but Olivia ignored her chatter. Her mother seemed to be so happy planning her only daughter's wedding. How could she ruin that for her? Instead of speaking, Olivia stood, walked away from the bed until her back was in full view of her mother, and let her dressing gown drop to the floor.

"*Mon due*," she gasped when she saw the bruising and swelling on her daughter's body. "Devaroe has done this to you?"

"Yes, Mother, this is how he consummated our betrothal." Olivia knelt and retrieved the discarded robe. "I cannot marry a man like that. I will not be like …" She let the words fall away into silence.

"You will not be like your beaten and crippled mother?" Marie stood and clutched at her cane for support. "You needn't be, daughter. Give him a son to inherit all of this," she waved her cane around the room and out the veranda, "and you needn't suffer him any longer."

"You can take your child and go where ever you please. Move yourselves to New Orleans or Paris. Educate your son to take over here when the time comes, but get yourself away from the depravities of your husband." Marie hobbled out onto the veranda, where a cool breeze blew inland from the Gulf, promising more severe weather later in the day. "I could never accomplish that. All my sons were born dead or dying. Had I been able to bear your father a living son, we would have left this place long ago."

"Mother." Olivia followed her mother out and took her frail hand. "I thought you stayed because you loved Father and wanted to please him."

"I loved your father with all my heart when we married, and I was certain he loved me, but I was a young and foolish girl then." Marie walked to the railing and leaned there looking out over the vast property of Sweet Rewards, the thin skirt of her light cotton day dress blowing in the breeze. "When you were born a girl, Armand was disappointed, but I thought I would have no problem giving him a son. You were conceived in our first month together, and the pregnancy went well. I had no idea you would be my only living child. I had to fulfill my duty as his wife and bear him a son and heir. Your father was a kind and loving man until that duel took his looks."

Marie tapped her cane against the railing and continued to gaze out across the dense green swamplands. "Then he became mean and took to drink. He began to blame himself when Georgia and his other dalliances produced only female children, too. I swore to myself that if I ever bore him a living son, I'd take us away from here." Marie reached into a pocket of her skirt and pulled out a small leather-bound book. She handed it back toward her daughter without looking away from the horizon.

"It's a bankbook for an account at the Lafayette Bank in New Orleans. I have been secreting funds there for decades now. You will find the account is also in your name, *ma Cherie*. When the time comes, there is more than enough money there to support you and your child handsomely. The townhouse in New Orleans is also deeded in your name. My father saw to that before his death." She smiled sadly as she stared out over Sweet Rewards. "He wanted you to have a legacy other than this mosquito-infested bog land, as he liked to call Sweet Rewards."

Olivia had little memory of her Grandfather La-Monte. Before her tenth birthday, he had died of yellow fever, but she and William had taken up residence in his townhouse in New Orleans soon after their wedding. Olivia loved the place that shared a courtyard with three other townhouses and stood close to the market square. From the veranda over the street, they could see the Gulf and smell the sea. Memories of coffee there with William, listening to the sea birds, and the bustling of the waking city were some of Olivia's most cherished.

Clutching the small book, a sliver of hope stabbed Olivia's heart. She could see herself living in the townhouse again with Magdalena. The family townhouse had survived the war with little damage, and her parents had paid to have the place renovated to use when the family went into the city. Now it sat waiting for her to return.

"*Ma Cherie,*" Marie said and took her daughter's trembling hand, "your father thinks we sold the townhouse after the War when you came home. There is no way Devaroe will ever know of its existence. I arranged through a friend to make it appear as though the property had been sold and took money from that account to give to your father as proceeds from the sale. He paid for the renovations after the war so we could sell it."

"But you, Georgia, Magdalena, and I have stayed there many times since the war," Olivia said, looking at her mother with a new appreciation. "Where did he think we were staying?"

"He always gave me money to stay at a hotel. That money went directly into the little book there for you. Armand does not deal with that bank and has no idea I have. My father banked there, and he was well respected."

"Mother," Olivia gasped and giggled. "I had no idea you could be so devious."

"My father's people came originally from Scotland, *Cherie*. It has ever been a hotbed of deception and intrigue." Marie laughed and turned back to face her daughter. "Now, we must begin planning this wedding and pray to God in Heaven that you conceived a son last night. You need not share your bed with the man again until after the wedding. As a matter of fact, I will protest to your father that I do not condone such activity under this roof. Your father may have betrothed you to the man, but you are not legally wed to him yet."

Olivia told her mother about Devaroe's note, and she scoffed at it. "Mr. Devaroe may protest all he likes, but he is still a guest under my roof and will abide by my wishes if he plans to remain here."

"And what about Father's wishes?" Olivia joined her mother at the railing and enjoyed the cool breeze. The scent of hot molasses carried on the wind from the processing plant reminded Olivia that she had not eaten yet today, and it was getting well into the afternoon. "Will you join me for lunch, Mother?"

"I've already had lunch, *ma petite,* but I will join you for tea and cakes on the patio. We can start a guest list for the wedding. When would you like to go to New Orleans for a dress? It may take a month to have one made." They both walked back into Olivia's room, where Marie picked up the pearl ring from the bedside table and handed it to her daughter. "Perhaps you should at least play the part of the hopeful bride." She arched a delicate eyebrow and grinned at her daughter.

Olivia rolled her eyes but took the ring and slid it onto her finger. "To Hell with buying a dress," Olivia hissed. "I will wear the Josephine dress for my wedding and say it holds fond memories for me because it was what I wore when I first met my betrothed." Olivia dressed quickly in a light cotton day dress.

Her mother smiled slyly. "I suppose if he can betroth you with a used ring, you can marry him in a used dress." Mother and daughter laughed together as they supported one another down the wide stairway to the Sweet Rewards mansion's foyer. Magdalena met them there just as Armand Thibodeaux and James Devaroe came through the front door.

"Magdalena, dear," Marie said to Olivia's maid, friend, and sister, "I am having your bed moved into my Olivia's room until the wedding." She gave her husband and Devaroe a withering glance and continued to the patio. "I will not have my daughter accused of being unchaste under my roof before her wedding." She winked at Olivia before turning to the two men. "Will you gentlemen care to join us for tea and cakes on the patio?"

Magdalena gave Olivia a questioning look before heading back to the kitchen to help her mother with

Marie's tea, and cakes served on the patio. Olivia smiled, followed her mother out through the heavy French doors, and took a seat at the round wrought-iron table.

You have more backbone than I gave you credit for, Mother.

Olivia watched her mother leaning on her cane as she walked.

It's a shame you never showed it sooner.

James Devaroe took the seat to the left of Olivia and lifted her hand to his lips, brushing it lightly. Noting she wore the ring, he smiled. "This ring belonged to my great-great-grandmother and is said to have been made from one of the first pearls to be brought to France from the Orient." He lifted Olivia's hand to show off the ring to her parents. "And these yellow diamonds come from a mine in India. They were gifts to the king himself from some potentate there."

"And what were your family's ties to the Royal House, Mr. Devaroe?" Marie asked as Magdalena brought out a tray laden with delicate porcelain cups. Saucers, a pot of tea, and a plate of cakes coated with a fine orange glaze also filled the tray. They would make her fingers sticky, but Olivia was ravenous and scooped up two of them to balance on the edges of her saucer next to her teacup.

Devaroe also took two of the sticky cakes and bit into one immediately. "My grandfather's grandfather on my father's side was a retainer to the king," he said with his mouth full, and he blew crumbs onto the table as he spoke.

"And how did your family, with their ties to the French royal family, manage to keep their heads during the Revolution?" Marie asked, furrowing her brow at his poor table manners.

"Like many families here in Louisiana, they had

fled to the new world before the heads began to roll into baskets in France. Yours, I believe, Mrs. Thibodeaux, fled to the Islands, while your husband's came here to the fertile swamps to produce the sweet gold we feast upon now." He popped the last bite of cake into his mouth and licked his fingers noisily.

"My great-grandfather moved down here from Canada to further his shipping concerns from the lakes and the rivers to include the high seas and the Islands," Devaroe said and sipped his tea. He furrowed his brow at the taste, took a silver flask from his pocket, and added something to the tea.

"Mr. Montrose was correct, of course, when he said I come from a family of pirates," Devaroe continued with a grin. "Much of my family fortune came from taking English and Spanish transport ships in the Caribbean. It was all quite legal and sanctioned by the government. We held privateering licenses from first the French and then from the real pirates in Washington." Armand joined him in a chuckle.

Devaroe smiled and bit into another cake. All the while, he held tight to Olivia's left hand with his right. She tried a few times to move it, but he held it in a vise-like grip. He seemed to be trying to let her know she belonged to him now and could not escape. He rotated his thumb over the iridescent pearl on the betrothal ring until the band cut into the soft flesh of Olivia's finger.

She finally relaxed her hand in his, and he took the pressure off the ring and her throbbing finger. Georgia brought out another pot of tea and bent to whisper something in Marie's ear. Marie smiled up at her. Georgia nodded and left.

"The boys have moved Magdalena's bed and bureau into your room, *ma Cherie*. Your honor is now safe," she said, giving Devaroe a black stare. "I will not have the neighbors slandering you at your wedding." Marie smiled sweetly at her husband, who sat glowering at her across the small table. "Olivia has decided to wear the beautiful Josephine dress that she met our Mr. Devaroe in as her wedding dress, so we will not need to wait for a seamstress to take weeks. I think we can have all the preparations made for a wedding two or three weeks from Saturday if that is agreeable with you, Mr. Devaroe."

He jerked his head around to look at Marie in surprise. "Of course, it is absolutely agreeable, Mrs. Thibodeaux." He lifted Olivia's hand to his lips and kissed it with a triumphant smile in his eyes. "I would wed her tomorrow if I could."

"I'm sure you would, Mr. Devaroe," Marie said and winked mischievously at her daughter. "I'm sure you would."

❧

James's mind roiled as he sat at the table with Olivia's hand in his. What had she told the old crone to ban him from her room and move her mulatto sister into her room?

We'll marry that little bitch off to one of the field hands and find Olivia a proper maid once we are married. I have no idea how Olivia can countenance her father's nigger git like that. It has to be humiliating, and I'll not have it in my home.

Two weeks after the hand-scribed invitations were delivered by house stewards of the Thibodeaux household, Olivia and Magdalena, who were rarely separated now, walked down the path together through the shady woods toward the pond with the dock. The hot late spring had turned into a hotter early summer in the Southern Louisiana bayous, and the only relief that anyone could find outside the sweltering house was in the open air of the shaded woodlands.

Olivia and her sister fanned away relentless hordes of buzzing mosquitos with their silk fans, to not much avail. Olivia slapped at her neck and Magdalena her arms.

"I hate these damned little bastards," Magdalena swore as she slapped Olivia's back, squashing a blood-filled insect going in for another bite. "The summer has just started, and I'm already wishin' for winter."

"I most certainly agree." Olivia swatted another with her fan as they neared the dock on the small pond, swollen from its normal banks by the recent rains. "I hope it cools a little for the wedding next weekend." On the dock, Olivia kicked off her slippers and hiked up her skirts above her knees before squatting to sit on the old boards of the pier. She dropped her feet into the green water of the pond and sighed as the cool water engulfed her legs.

"We're gonna be gator bait swingin' our legs in the water like this." Magdalena dropped down next to her sister and splashed her feet in the water, sending up a cooling spray of droplets onto both of them.

"Roy says he hasn't seen signs of a gator in this pond in years. Do you see any wallows or slides?" Olivia swung her arm around to indicate the pond's banks that showed no tell-tale signs of alligators sliding from them into the water. The big beasts tended to have regular spots where they sunned themselves and left a muddy trail where they went in and out of the water.

"Ouch!" Olivia suddenly jerked her left leg up out of the water to reveal a tiny circular welt on her calf. "Damned perch."

Magdalena began laughing but pulled one of her legs up with a welt of her own. "We just food for everything today, it seems, Livvy. Keep your legs movin', and they won't get ya." Magdalena dipped her hand into the pond and sent an arc of water flying up toward her sister, who jumped and squealed with delight when the cool liquid hit her face and shoulders. She bent and did the same. Soon both young women sat wet from head to waist and laughing like little children.

In the throes of their playful distraction, they did not see or hear James Devaroe come down the path to the pond. It was not until they felt the treads of his boots on the wooden planks that they knew they no longer had the pond to themselves.

"I see you ladies have found a relief from this miserable heat. May I join you?" He kicked off his short boots, rolled up his trousers to his knees, and sat down next to Olivia, using her shoulder as a crutch until he was down. He slid his hand down to encircle her waist and pulled her closer to him. They'd had little time to be alone or close to one another since the night of their betrothal.

"I have missed you," he whispered into her ear before nipping the lobe hard enough to make her jerk away. That made him laugh, and when Olivia glanced over, she could see a bulge growing in the front of his trousers. "Why don't we really cool off?" He laughed and pushed her into the water.

Magdalena, sitting close to her sister, grabbed for her when she heard Olivia give a startled gasp and begin going off the weathered old boards. Olivia's momentum pulled Magdalena with her as she went off the dock into the murky green water of the little pond. They could hear Devaroe laughing wildly as they sank into the pond. Their skirts became heavy in the water and pulled them both down until their naked toes touched the slippery muck at the bottom of the shallow pond.

Olivia held her breath and blew air through her nose to keep the water out. She pushed up with her toes but rose slowly in her heavy, wet skirt and petticoat. Magdalena did the same, and soon their heads broke the water, and they reached for the edge of the dock to pull themselves up. Devaroe, still laughing maniacally, offered Olivia his hand. She took it, but instead of using it to pull herself out of the water, she gave it a mighty tug and sent the laughing Devaroe head-first into the pond with them.

Magdalena heaved herself up onto the dock and tried to help Olivia. Still, before she could get her sister up, a strong hand grabbed Olivia and pulled her back into the water, leaving Magdalena alone, open-mouthed, on the old planks.

In the water, Devaroe pulled Olivia to him and kissed her mouth hard. He shoved his tongue between her lips and teeth until it found hers and twined around it with ferocity. He tasted of stale tobacco and whisky. He held her tight around the waist with one hand while with the other, he pulled up her wet skirts until he found her bloomers, which he ripped away so he could get his hand between her legs and find his prize.

I have been longing for this. It has been too long since our night together. You need a reminder that you belong to me now.

Olivia did not struggle against him, allowing wandering fingers into her beneath the green waters of the pond while Magdalena looked on from the safety of the old dock. Devaroe pushed her toward the pilings until Olivia's back rested against old wood, slick with green slime. He continued to kiss her with her hair getting tangled and pulled in the splintered old cypress posts holding up the dock. He took his hand out of her, and Olivia could feel him unbuttoning his wet trousers to release his hard cock into the water.

She felt him pushing her skirts up again and pulling her legs up until they encircled his waist. With one quick shove, he was inside her. He broke the seal he had on her mouth and gave a loud grunt of pleasure as he entered her. He tried to get to her breasts, but her bodice's fabric clung tight to her, and no matter how hard he tugged, the buttons fastening her dress in the back would not give. In mad frustration, he bit into her neck and sucked at it painfully while he pounded into her under the water. He shoved her bare butt cheeks against the old wood of the slime-coated piling.

Your mother may have thought to keep you from me, but you are mine now, Olivia, and she'll not deny me.

Though she felt violated, Olivia's body reacted of its own accord, and soon she found herself clenching his cock inside her and arching into his thrusts. She reluctantly invited him into her and shivered with pleasure as he slid over that tender spot between her thighs, and she exploded with a loud gasp of released, frustrating pleasure. She could not help herself, pulled him into her, and returned his kisses until he too groaned and shoved her one last time into the old post.

Withering out of her, his cock and most of his fluids floated out into the murky waters of the pond. "You see, *Cherie*, we are excellent together," he breathed into her ear before releasing his grip on her legs and back-paddling into the water as he rebuttoned his trousers.

Olivia, her torn bloomers long gone somewhere at the bottom of the pond, turned to heft herself back up onto the dock. Magdalena bent and tugged at her shoulder to help her up, and soon Olivia sat, a soggy mess, on the edge of the pier. Devaroe swam over to her and reached up for her to take his hand.

Unsure if she could trust him not to pull her back into the water, Olivia stretched out her left hand to him. He grabbed it but did not get a good grasp, and with both their hands still wet, he slipped free. In doing so, Devaroe pulled the pearl ring from Olivia's wet finger. The three of them watched it fall into the green depths of the pond. Devaroe's eyes went wide with the loss of his valued family heirloom, and he immediately dove in after it.

Olivia did not know what to feel. She felt sorrow at the loss of a treasured family jewel but not sorry for any loss to her. The ring meant nothing to her. She watched Devaroe come up for air and dive down again a dozen times before he finally gave up and pushed himself up on the deck next to her. She did not say anything, and neither did Magdalena, who sat next to her wringing out her drenched hair.

After a few silent moments, Devaroe grabbed Olivia's shoulders, turned her toward him, and scowled into Olivia's eyes. "You did that on purpose, you little pampered bitch," he seethed. "If you wanted a new ring, why didn't you just say so?" He swung his arm and hit the post of the old dock with such force. Olivia flinched away from him and went flying off the dock into the water. She hit her face on the post and landed in the water with a splash that drenched both Devaroe and a wide-eyed, stunned Magdalena.

Devaroe turned and stormed off the dock and back up the path toward the house carrying his boots and leaving Olivia flailing in the water.

I can't believe she allowed my ring to drop into the pond. She's a foolish, spoiled child. Armand's business and this horrible swampland are not worth her foolishness.

Magdalena stretched an arm out to her from the old wooden dock. "Come on, Livvy," Magdalena called, reaching for her flailing sister. Olivia righted herself in the water, still stunned by Devaroe's ridiculous accusations and dizzy from hitting her head. She swam slowly through the water and took Magdalena's outstretched hand. Olivia let her sister assist her back onto the old dock, where she slumped against her in silence.

"You alright, Livvy?" Magdalena wiped a trickle of blood from the corner of Olivia's mouth with her skirt. "That lip's gonna be a frightful mess for a day or two, and your face is gonna be bruised somethin' fierce for a while. We better get you back to your room and keep you hid from your Mammy for a while."

Magdalena helped Olivia unsteadily to her feet. They walked with a shaking Olivia being held by her sister, both fighting sodden skirts up the slippery path and shooing away mosquitos with their fans. "That woman might take this kind of treatment by Daddy, but she's not gonna 'bide it for her daughter even if it be from the rich riverboat man Daddy wants you to marry. She's probably gonna shoot that riverboat man if she sees you like this."

Olivia gave her sister a half-hearted laugh at the thought of her mother going after Devaroe with her gun. "That's not Mother's style. She's more likely to spike his bourbon with ground castor beans or sprinkle it on his cakes at tea time."

"That'd do it for certain." Magdalena laughed as she slowed at the edge of the lawn to see that the way was clear, and Marie Thibodeaux was not sitting in her chair enjoying the shade of the patio. "You got any of them castor beans in your medicine box, Liv? I might just pound me up some and dose that river-boat man myself. He ain't nothin' but a foul-mouthed son-of-a-bitch. He the one that pulled that ring off your finger and dropped it, not you."

They entered the house without speaking and slogged their way up the stairs in their clinging, wet skirts to Olivia's room, where Magdalena now also resided. She locked the door after they entered, and they began shedding their wet clothes. She wrapped herself in a dry dressing gown, took her wet things out, and draped them over the railing of the veranda to dry before going back in and picking up Olivia's and doing the same with them.

Olivia went into her privy closet and stared at her aching face in the mirror over her vanity. Her lip bled from a swollen split on the right side, and her cheek looked blue and swollen, as well. Olivia touched it gingerly and winced. She knew there would be no hiding it for a few days until the swelling went down and shook her head in disgust at James Devaroe.

He's no better than Daddy, and I'll not have it.

At the little cabinet where Olivia kept her supply of medicinals, she took out a blue glass jar containing yarrow salve and dabbed some of it on her split lip. The balm would help heal the wound and ease the swelling. After returning the salve to the cabinet, Olivia went out to the veranda with her comb to attempt to untangle her hair and comb out all the slimy, green moss from the dock's pillar.

As she combed her hair, Olivia could not keep from thinking of Devaroe between her legs. The man satisfied her that she could not deny. The sting of the salve on her lip reminded her of his brutal nature, however.

He's just like Daddy, and I will not be treated the way Mother has been treated all these years. I know that all men are not this way. William was so gentle and kind. Are there no more like him in this God-forsaken Louisiana?

Olivia sat, combing her hair up and over her head, when her father began pounding on her door and demanding she open it to let him in. Magdalena opened the door, and he shoved his way past her to join Olivia on the veranda. He grabbed Olivia by the hair she had combed forward and yanked her head back to look at her face.

"What in Hell's name did you go and do, Olivia Marie? Your husband is packing his clothes to leave Sweet Rewards before your damned wedding ceremony."

"I didn't *do* anything, Father," Olivia retorted hotly. "We were cooling off in the pond, and when he grabbed my hand, the ring came off and fell in the water."

Armand Thibodeaux twisted and pulled his daughter's hair harder. "He says you took off the ring and *threw* it at him in the water."

"She done no such thing, sir," Magdalena said from inside the room.

"You stay out of this, girl." He pulled Olivia's hair again, bringing hot tears to her eyes. "This is between my fool daughter and me."

"Well, just you look at your fool daughter's face and see what that riverboat man done to her, and he be the one that pulled off that ring and let it drop, not Miss Livvy," Magdalena uncharacteristically stormed at their father.

Armand Thibodeaux walked around to take a good look at Olivia's face and noted the bluing of her cheek and the swollen, bloodied lip. "I suppose you've already gotten the throttling you deserve, Olivia," he said and let go of her hair, allowing it to fall once more to cover her battered face. "Stay in your damned room, though." He stalked through the room and yanked open the door. "I don't want your mother seeing you in this state. She is already in a fitful state over this whole wedding business," he told Olivia and slammed the door behind him.

Olivia sat in the chair with her hair a mess around her face and tears washing down her bruised cheek. She cried just like she had when her father had scolded or whipped her as a child.

If that son-of-a-bitch is leaving Sweet Rewards, then so am I. I'll go to New Orleans to the townhouse. What a bastard, Olivia thought, but she didn't know if she thought it about Devaroe or her single-minded father.

❧ 8 ❧

James Devaroe did leave Sweet Rewards, even with her father threatening breach of contract lawsuits against him. The man left in a huff, cursing Olivia with every breath. She and Magdalena heard him go as they leaned over the railing of the veranda and laughed at their father chasing after Devaroe, screaming and waving his arms in fury.

I can't get away from this misbegotten place fast enough.

Devaroe eased his horse into a walk after he was out of Sweet Rewards' sight, and certain Armand was not following him. It would be dark in a few hours, but he remembered passing a couple of inns just south of the main highway back to New Orleans. He was certain he could make it to one of them before nightfall.

He slowed his mount when he saw a gang of men crossing the road from a stand of cane to another. A man on horseback followed them and stopped in the road when he saw Devaroe. As he drew closer, the man behind the workmen recognized him, and Devaroe saw a smirking grin spread across his face.

"Did Olivia finally come to her senses and send your pirating ass on its way, Devaroe?" Simon Montrose said with a chuckle. "I'm sure Armand will press her to marry me now. He wants an heir." Montrose smirked. "And the wedding invitations have already been sent out. I'll ride over there this very afternoon and make my case. There's no sense wasting all the wedding food. I'm sure he's already laid by." Montrose cackled.

Anger and jealousy surged through Devaroe as he scowled at the pudgy man astride the white horse. He knew the man was right, and Armand would probably force Olivia into a marriage with this fool if he made a good case. Devaroe saw Olivia's gentle eyes and suddenly couldn't bear the idea of this fool atop her.

"I'm just going into my offices in N'Orleans to deal with some business matters before my wedding next weekend." He smiled at Montrose. "I have to make a quick trip of it," he said and brought a hand down to his crotch. "I've got to get back to attend to Olivia. Armand is, indeed, in a hurry for that heir. My betrothal night and every night since have fairly worn my little man out in the attempt."

"You're a cad, Devaroe," Montrose sneered. "She deserves better."

"You mean you?" Devaroe said in a mocking tone. "You wouldn't last a night under Olivia Montgomery's tender mercies. That woman would wear your little cock down to a nub." It was now Devaroe's turn to cackle as Montrose's face went pale with rage.

"You'll pay for that, pirate," Montrose seethed. "Take him," Montrose yelled and motioned to his field hands. "He's yours to do with as you please, and then leave him in the ditch for the scavengers."

Negroes rushed toward Devaroe and pulled him from his horse. They delivered punches and kicks, spit on him, and pulled off his boots and his jacket. Devaroe could hear Montrose's cackling laugh until a kick to his head sent him into a black abyss of pain-less relief.

⬥⬥⬥

"Well, I guess we gonna have to send out uninvites to that wedding," Magdalena said with a giggle.

"That suits me just fine," Olivia snapped as she dried her tears, combed back her hair, and stood up. "Pack our bags, Magda. We're going to New Orleans."

"That sounds like fun," Magdalena sighed. "How many days you want me to pack for us, two or three?"

"Pack it all," Olivia stormed. "We're leaving this God-forsaken swamp for good." Olivia walked to her wardrobe and began tossing dresses onto the bed. She emptied it except for the chiffon Josephine gown. That she left hanging and slammed the wardrobe doors.

When they finished, there were four cases stuffed almost past the point of buckling shut. The keys to the townhouse and the leather bankbook rested at the bottom of Olivia's satchel along with her jewelry, her personal stationery, a corked bottle of ink, her pens, and her silver-framed photo of William.

Olivia sent Magdalena to tell the groom to have the old buggy hitched and ready for them at first light in the morning. She wanted to get as far away from Sweet Rewards as she possibly could tomorrow.

Magdalena brought their supper up to their room, and Olivia gingerly ate the ham, green beans, and cornbread with the enthusiasm of an inmate to be released from her prison. Magdalena, who had told her mother about their departure, did not enjoy her meal quite as much.

"My Mammy ain't none too happy about this movin' away and not tellin' the Misses about it. She thinks it cruel and mean not to let your Mammy say a proper goodbye."

"My Mother will understand completely. I've left a detailed note for her."

"A note," Magdalena scoffed, "ain't no proper kiss and hug goodbye."

"It will suffice," Olivia said and tossed her dressing gown on the bed. "I am going to have a bath. The water should be cool enough by now. You didn't pack away my soap and sponge, did you?"

"No, ma'am, Miss Livvy, ma'am, they be right there with your tub." Magdalena laughed as she put the dirty dishes on the tray to take back to the kitchen.

"Oh, hush up," Olivia snapped, surly, at her sister as she stepped into the tub. "You know I don't condone that kind of talk in my room."

"Yes, ma'am, Miss Livvy, ma'am." She laughed and ducked out the door as Olivia's wet sponge came flying at her to land with a wet squish on the closing door and slide to the floor with a plop.

Olivia smiled at her sister's sarcastic nature and rested her head on the edge of the white porcelain tub, relaxing. The thought of Devaroe leaving in a huff amused her, and she smiled. Then the thought of him pumping into her there in the pond kindled overwhelming warmth between her legs again. There was no getting around it, that man set her loins on fire.

Well, he is gone now, and life will go on at Sweet Rewards, but it will have to go on without me.

Olivia lowered her hand down between her legs to massage the throbbing bulb until she experienced those delicious explosive waves of pleasure that made her groan and shiver in her warm bath. Olivia could not ignore his violent tendencies when her lip started throbbing too. The vicious punch on the dock had both surprised and stunned her.

We had just made love. How could he possibly have been so vicious toward me after that?

She shook her head and slid under the water to wet her hair for washing. The orange blossom-scented soap both relaxed and soothed her. Olivia used the sweet-smelling bar to lather her head until she'd piled all her black locks in a huge coil on top of her head. Her head, still tender from her father's assault, ached and stung. She massaged it and made certain the soap got down to the scalp to dislodge any of the slimy green moss that may have been deposited there earlier.

Olivia slid down beneath the tepid water again and ran her fingers through her hair to get out the soap, though she loved the scent it left behind if she didn't get it all. With her hair free of soap, Olivia pulled herself up in the tub and jumped with a start to see her mother standing over her.

"Did you honestly think you could sneak away from here without me knowing about it, *Cherie?*" Marie handed her daughter a towel and gasped when she saw the swollen lip and blue cheek. "Devaroe?"

Olivia nodded, stepped out of the tub, and fell into her mother's arms sobbing. "I am so very sorry, *ma mere.* I know you and Georgia have been working late into the nights to put together this wedding, and now I have gone and ruined it." Olivia wrapped her arms around her mother and rested her wet head on her shoulder.

"Hush now, daughter, nothing has been done that cannot be undone." Marie led her sobbing daughter to the bed to sit. Olivia saw her looking at the pile of bulging cases and choked off a sob. "I am not here to stop you," Marie said in a soothing whisper. "I am here to tell you that you need not worry about your father in this matter. I have sent him off to drink and play cards in St. Johns. He will be there all night and well into tomorrow morning with one of his whores."

Marie used the towel to dry Olivia's back and wrapped it around her dripping hair. She kissed her daughter's cheek with soft, warm lips that Olivia remembered from her childhood, soothing her after a skinned knee or a spanking from her father.

"I will tell him you have gone off in shame over losing Devaroe and disappointing him. That will feed his oversized ego until you can get safely away and ensconced in the townhouse. I will tell him you have gone to stay with your school friend in Shreveport."

"Thank you, Mother," Olivia said, wiping her face with the end of the towel. "We will leave at first light and hopefully make it into New Orleans before it gets too dark. If not, there are several good inns along the way."

"You must be cautious of bandits along the way, *ma Cherie*. I have heard there are roving bands of freed slaves lying in wait for unsuspecting travelers. Here, take this," Marie said and put a small Derringer into Olivia's hand. "I have loaded it, and here is more ammunition and the thigh holster." She laid a leather drawstring bag in Olivia's lap. "You remember how to load it?"

"Yes, Mother," Olivia sighed, "you've spent hours with my loading and reloading the damned thing."

"I know," Marie said uneasily, "but promise me you will keep it on your person and not in some bag packed in the back of the carriage. Wear your special traveling skirt." Marie stood, leaning on her cane. She reached out, lifted her daughter's head with small, frail hand, and planted a kiss on Olivia's damp forehead. "I love you, *ma Cherie;* you are my only living child. I cherish you in my heart, but it is time for you to move on. Go to New Orleans, make a home for yourself in the townhouse, go to parties and the opera, meet a man you can love, and perhaps give me a grandchild to hold before I die." Marie brushed tears from her cheek, turned, and left her daughter sitting on her bed quietly weeping.

❅ 9 ❅

Olivia looked out over Sweet Rewards from her veranda for what she hoped would be one last time. The early morning fog, not yet burned off by the relentless summer sun, crept across the grounds, wrapping its wispy tendrils around trees and bushes. The fog mixed with the Spanish moss hanging from the old trees gave the place an ethereal glow that had scared her as a child after hearing Georgia's stories about the ghosts of witches and murdered women who haunted the bayou.

This morning Olivia stared at the vast grounds with its creeping fog and hanging moss and felt excited to be leaving it. She looked out over the acres of Sweet Rewards to etch a picture of it in her mind. The early morning breeze carried the scent of summer jasmine, honeysuckle, and molasses. Olivia closed her eyes and inhaled that memory too.

The sound of Jimbo coming in to pick up the last two cases to take to the buggy jolted Olivia out of her silent vigil.

"These is the last two cases, Miss Livvy. The buggy be ready when I get them stowed," the burly groom told her and picked up the heavy leather cases. He walked out the door to carry them down to the waiting buggy below.

Olivia followed him in her dark red poplin traveling suit. She carried a straw bonnet to put on when the sun came out and her personal leather bag that she would stow by her feet as it carried what cash money she had, the bank book, her jewelry, and the key to her lovely townhouse. The little gun she had strapped to her thigh in a holster, concealed by her skirt but easily fetched through a false pocket.

The design had been crafted by her mother years ago for long trips on the road. The swamps bred their own pirates. The wild men's boats, just little skiffs that they could easily maneuver through the trees in the shallow waters, were pirate ships. The men would pilot their small boats close to the roads and silently lie waiting for unsuspecting travelers.

Olivia remembered hearing tales of travelers being robbed, beaten, and murdered along the muddy track from St. Johns to the main highway into New Orleans. Olivia's mother worried about roving bands of freed Negroes, but Olivia had heard these stories long before the Negroes had been freed. She knew these scoundrels were white and always had been. She ran her hand over her skirt and felt the security of the little Derringer secreted there.

Olivia walked through the meandering mist still clinging to the ground and climbed into the old buggy, heavily laden with her and Magdalena's luggage. She heard the wailing of Georgia and knew Magdalena would soon be joining her. In a coffee-brown traveling suit much darker than her skin and carrying a folded parasol, Magdalena climbed up into the seat beside Olivia.

"Let's get this travelin' act movin'," Magdalena

said as she wiped tears from her face and blew her nose on a clean cotton handkerchief.

Olivia took the reins hooked to Old Blue, the dappled-gray horse she and William had bought as a colt soon after marrying. William, who knew his horse flesh, had said the colt would serve them for many years. As it turned out, he never really served William, but Olivia loved and pampered him. Blue was one of the only things she had left of William, and after the past few days, she needed to feel close to her late husband again. After Devaroe's departure, Olivia had returned the narrow, gold wedding band placed there by William all those years ago to her finger. She was Mrs. William Tyler Montgomery and always would be.

I don't know; whatever gave me the idea I could ever be anything else.

They traveled steadily along the muddy, rutted track from Sweet Rewards toward the main road north to the King's Highway that led into New Orleans. The fog burned off by nine, and the sun came out to scorch them through bright cloudless, cerulean blue skies.

Olivia pulled to a stop, got her bonnet from behind her seat, and tied it on. Thus far, they had driven directly into the bright morning sun for most of their trip, but soon they would reach the track north, and she could stop squinting. Luckily the road was overhung, for the most part, by big trees that shaded the women, but the northern track was edged by cane and rice fields, with scant relief from the hot Louisiana sun.

About a mile from the intersection of the two roads, Olivia noticed something strange in the weeds ahead of her by the road. As she neared what looked like a roll of cloth, Olivia pulled gently on Blue's reins to slow him.

"Will you go and see what that is, Magda," Olivia asked her sister, who sat on the side of the buggy where the object lay. They neared it, and Olivia swore she saw movement. Perhaps it was nothing more than an old tarp with an animal nesting beneath it.

Olivia scanned both sides of the track, looking closely into the thick brush along the way. The road agents were said to entrap travelers passing by with something laid out to slow them down. As they neared the object, it became clear to Olivia that it was no discarded tarp. The distinct form of shoeless male feet and legs in trousers lay there motionless in the thick weeds.

Olivia stared intently into the bushes but saw no signs of humans there. She even looked up into the high limbs of old oaks in case they hid there, ready to jump down on them. She pulled Blue to a halt, and Magdalena jumped down out of the buggy and ran to the body.

With a startled expression, Magdalena shouted up to her, "It be that riverboat man, Livvy, and he's in a bad way. You better come take a look. I don't think he dead, but he beat up really bad."

Olivia jumped down and ran around Blue. She gave him a quick pat on the muzzle as she passed to reassure him. Lying there in the mud and weeds, Olivia saw, was James Devaroe. Evidently, he had not been as vigilant as she while traveling down this lonely path. Along with his boots, he was also missing his hat, jacket, and gold cuff links. That silver flask probably was not in his vest pocket either.

Magdalena knelt on one side of Devaroe and

Olivia on the other. Purple stained his eyes, which were swollen shut, and he had bruises and knuckle scrapes on both his cheeks. His lips trickled blood down his stubbled chin and looked like a rose blossom. They were red from his broken and bleeding nose and swollen. Olivia could see boot prints on his white silk shirt, and she knew he had suffered several vicious kicks and stomps to his torso.

She and Magdalena managed to roll Devaroe over onto his back, and Olivia, who had helped in a hospital during the war, carefully ran her hands over his bruised sides to check for broken ribs. They all felt intact, but that did not mean there were not cracks she couldn't feel.

"From the look of these bruises," Olivia said to her sister as she felt for breaks again. "I bet he has some cracked ribs. They are too bad to have not done some serious damage."

Now it was Magdalena peering into the wooded hedges for bandits. "We better get him up in the buggy, if we can, before the bastards come back."

"James." Olivia patted his bruised face to tried and wake him. "Magda, get me the canteen, please." When it came, Olivia put the opening to his mouth and tried to get some water through his swollen lips. She took the opportunity and ran her hands over his face to check for broken bones there as well. The nose definitely felt broken, and she eased the notch of the damaged cartilage back into place and cringed at the sound of the gristle scraping together beneath the skin.

The pain of that brought Devaroe around, and his eyes fluttered open as far as they could through the swelling. Olivia could not tell whether he recognized her or not, but she repeated his name and offered the canteen again. This time he parted his lips with a painful moan and accepted the water. Olivia warned him to swallow carefully so he wouldn't choke.

"James, do you think you can get up? We need to get you into the buggy." Olivia and Magdalena helped him to sit, but his head fell over as he swooned again from the pain of his many injuries. They couldn't just sit there holding him all afternoon, so Olivia began dumping the contents of the canteen over his head.

That revived him enough that they could get him, unsteadily, to his feet and walk him to the buggy. Both held him up by the waist of his dirty, torn trousers.

"Let's gets him up in the seat with you, Livvy. I'll ride in the back on the cases," Magdalena said and helped heave the heavy man up into the seat of the buggy. She then climbed up into the crowded back compartment with their luggage. Olivia returned to her seat and reached over to make certain Devaroe sat securely on the buggy's padded bench seat before picking up the reins and getting Blue moving once more.

"Where are we gonna take him?" Magdalena called from the back.

Olivia turned the buggy around in the narrow track. "Back to Sweet Rewards, I guess. The only other place nearby is Montrose's house, and I am *not* going there," Olivia said. "Hold on tight, Magda. I'm going to run Blue as fast as I can to get us back before too long. I don't know how long he can remain sitting up."

"Give Blue the reins, Liv. I'll hold on." Magdalena secured herself amongst the luggage and held tight to the back of the seat and the outer edge of the little buggy

Olivia slapped the reins on Blue's dappled behind, and the horse took off at a trot. He bounced everyone and everything in the buggy. A few times, Olivia had to reach out with her right arm to pull Devaroe back from the edge of the buggy. Finally, she let the man slump over onto her shoulder while she did her best to keep them out of major mud holes and ruts. Blue did an excellent job of steering them around the dangers, but after almost half an hour at the fast pace in the hot afternoon sun, the horse began to lather.

Just past the turn into the Montrose estate, Olivia had to slow Blue. A group of people stood in the road ahead, blocking her way. They didn't look like highwaymen. Olivia thought they must be field workers on their way home, but they did not part for her, and she had to stop.

Behind the dozen Negro men surrounding the buggy now sat a stout, pale man wearing a wide-brimmed straw hat on a white horse. When he began laughing, she recognized Simon Montrose.

"Well, Olivia dear," he sneered in a high nasal voice, "I see you've found and collected your wayward fiancé."

"You did this to him, Simon, and just left him by the side of the road to die like an animal?" Olivia raged at the scurrilous man on the horse, trying to look taller in the saddle than he actually was.

"Now, don't get your bloomers in a twist over some worthless pretender." Montrose chortled. "My proud family can trace its roots back to the throne of Louis XIV."

"What were they, groundskeepers, stable hands, or muckrakers in the midden pits at Versailles?" Olivia sneered.

Montrose rode up to the buggy, grabbed Olivia

by the hair, and pushed off her wind-blown bonnet. "How dare you insult my family name, you spoiled little puffed-up tart." He pulled his booted foot out of the stirrup and kicked Olivia solidly in the chest between her breasts. She gasped as the vicious kick surprised her and temporarily knocked the breath from her lungs.

When her breathing came back to her, Olivia could hear Magdalena screaming curses as she fought from behind the buggy. Men laughed and called out lascivious comments to their fellow attackers. Olivia could hear fabric ripping and the sound of hands slapping bare flesh.

Soon Magdalena quieted, but the hooting and laughing of the men behind the buggy continued. Olivia could only imagine the defiling her sister must be enduring at the hands of Montrose's band of field hands.

Montrose sat watching what was going on in the road behind the buggy and laughed maniacally. "I hear that nigger bitch is your sister, Olivia." He laughed at Olivia, who was snaking her hand into the false pocket of her skirt. "If you fuck as nice as it looks like she does, you and I will have a fine marriage indeed."

"I seriously doubt that," Olivia said as she raised the little pistol and aimed it at Montrose's midsection. His eyes grew wide at the sight of the little double-barreled gun, and he began backing his horse away. "Call off your dogs, Simon, or I'm going to blow a hole in your belly big enough to jump through."

Devaroe, who still had his head on her shoulder, whispered hoarsely in her ear, "Shoot the snarling bitch, and the pups will run away."

"Call them off, Simon, or I'll shoot you. I swear, I will."

"Now Olivia, my sweet, you wouldn't harm your future husband before he gets a chance to taste that sweet cunny of yo …"

He didn't get the chance to finish his crude sentence as his guts began falling out of his belly onto his saddle from the double-barreled shot from the little gun. The laughter from behind the buggy turned to silence after the loud pistol blast and then to the sound of running feet as Olivia jumped from the buggy and stood, waving the pistol in their direction.

She watched the Negro workers go running off toward Montrose House, some of them struggling to hold up their pants as they fled. Olivia rushed from the buggy to kneel at Magdalena's side. She lay practically naked in the soupy red mud of the road, her clothes torn and haphazardly pushed around so the men could touch her bosoms and get between her wide-spread legs.

"Magda." Olivia wept at seeing her beloved sister in such a state.

Magdalena pushed herself up on one elbow and glanced around at her ripped clothes. "I'm gonna kill me some cock-sucking cane-field nigger sons-of-bitches." She rolled and pushed up onto her knees in the mud, and Olivia stood to help her up. When Magdalena got to her feet, her muddy petticoat fell from her waist, where her attackers had pushed up to reveal her curly black nest.

Magdalena picked up her torn, muddy camisole and put it back on. Unable to button it because the men had popped all of them off to get to her bosoms, she just tied it at the top and held it together with her muddy, shaking hands. Her fingers were bloody where the nails had broken off to the quick in the struggle with her attackers. Olivia picked up the remnants of the brown suit and handed them to her sister, who had climbed awkwardly back into the cramped rear of the buggy.

"I see you done got *your* cocksucker," she snorted a laugh, referring to Montrose slumped and bloody but still mounted in his saddle.

When she walked back to get in the buggy again, Olivia slapped the white horse, now streaked red and brown with dribbling blood and gore down its sides. She smacked it hard on its rump, and it headed back toward his stable at Montrose House at full gallop.

Olivia watched Simon Montrose's body shift and bounce in the saddle with trailing entrails, flinging blood and filth about the frightened steed as it ran. Somehow, the body managed to stay on the horse as it rounded the turn to the plantation.

Run on home to daddy, Simon. I don't think he'll be able to fix this one for you.

Olivia took her seat and set Blue to a trot once more. With still an hour until dusk, the buggy stopped in front of Sweet Rewards, and Jimbo, their groom, came running at the sight of Blue in a lather. He began yelling, and soon it seemed like the whole plantation milled around their buggy.

Jimbo rushed to help Magdalena down from the buggy's back with great care and carried her into the house and up the stairs. Some of the hands unharnessed Blue and walked him back to the stables, where Olivia knew he would be rubbed down until he was dry and then be rubbed with liniment to ease his sore muscles.

Devaroe was helped out of the buggy and taken into the house, where Olivia knew he too would be well attended. Her bleary-eyed father and anxious mother met her on the porch.

"What is this all about, Olivia? I thought you were going to Shreveport. How did your sister end up in such a state?" her father asked, surprising Olivia with the concern in his voice for his other daughter. "And what are you doing with James?"

"I *was* going to Shreveport," Olivia said with dry sarcasm, "but Mother said you were ever so distraught over losing yet another prospective husband for me. I went out and found the son-of-a-bitch and dragged him back here. As you can see, he put up a bit of a fuss, and I had to get a little rough with him." She winked at her mother, who stood behind Armand Thibodeaux, doing her best to hold in a giggle.

"I had to be a little forceful with him when he put up a fight about coming back," Olivia continued as she walked up beneath the columned balcony of the shady porch. "It may be all for naught, though," she said as she pulled open the heavy oak front door. "I killed Simon Montrose." Olivia handed her mother the little Derringer while her father stood looking on in shocked amazement with his eyes wide and his mouth opening and closing like a catfish lying on a dry bank.

The next two weeks blurred in Olivia's mind. Magdalena recovered in Olivia's room. She woke many nights listening to her sister sobbing into her pillows. After her first attempt to console her and Magda slapping away, Olivia just let Magdalena cry it out. Rage and a sense of helplessness possessed her poor sister that Olivia could do nothing to assuage. Olivia hoped none of those men ever got near Magdalena, who now carried a large knife strapped to her waist.

James Devaroe recovered slowly in the guest suite down the hall. The doctor brought out from St. Johns had diagnosed him with severely bruised and several cracked ribs. He'd lost a couple of teeth, and his attackers had cracked his jawbone on the right side of his head. The old doctor told them the men had severely bruised one of Devaroe's kidneys with their many vicious kicks as well. The white-haired doctor wrapped Devaroe's torso tightly and recommended a soft diet and lots of water. Devaroe did not like his restriction of alcohol for two weeks, but Olivia brought a flask to him anyhow to help ease his pain.

She slipped into his room on the fifth night after their return and sat down in the chair next to his bed.

"I told you before that you'd never make it as a scout," he whispered with a hoarse laugh.

"I didn't mean to wake you, but I brought you a gift," she said as she handed him the flask she'd bought in St. Johns the day before to replace the one he'd lost.

"You are truly an angel sent to me from Heaven, Mrs. Montgomery," he said and clumsily uncorked the flask he put immediately to his very swollen pink lips. Much of the bourbon never made it into his mouth, but Devaroe seemed to enjoy what did.

"Is your sister alright?" he asked her between painful sips.

"I don't know," Olivia sighed. "She cries at night and won't talk to me about it." Olivia sat quietly for a moment, thinking. "I think she is angry with me because I got to kill Montrose, and she didn't get a chance to kill any of the men who hurt her."

"She will work it out in time," Devaroe said confidently. "She's a strong woman and doesn't strike me as the type that chews on something for any length of time."

"She's carrying a really big knife now," Olivia told him as she took the empty flask from his hands.

He grabbed her hand, brought her wrist to his nose, and inhaled deeply. "Orange Blossom. Thank you for wearing it, Olivia." He kissed the wrist gently before dropping it. "And I hope none of those sons-of-bitches ever find themselves in a dark alley with your sweet sister."

"Hell," Olivia scoffed, "I hope she ends up in a dark alley with all of them, one at a time. I might even see if I can arrange it somehow."

"You're a hard woman, Mrs. Montgomery," Devaroe said with a painful chuckle.

The following night, Olivia returned to his side with another flask. "I probably shouldn't be doing this," she whispered as she handed it to him. "The doctor said you should have no liquor, but you are in so much pain. I don't think this little bit to help you sleep will hurt you overmuch."

"Neither do I," he said as he tipped up the flask and drank deeply. Olivia watched him and was relieved that she could ease his pain just a little.

Should I even give a good God damn after he hurt me the way he did? He is still a human being in pain. After spending all that time in the Army hospital, watching those boys suffer, I can't bear to see it.

Olivia walked to the bed and straightened the blankets around him. The heat in the room was stifling, so she did not cover him with them. The window stood open with cheesecloth tacked over it to keep out the mosquitos, but no breeze refreshed the hot room.

Devaroe took her hand, inhaled the fragrance at her wrist again, and gently kissed it with his bruised and swollen lips.

"Have they come for you over Montrose's death?" he asked with her wrist at his nose.

"Yes," Olivia whispered, "they came for me the next day, and we had to go into St. John's to see the magistrate. Father made them come up here and look at you and," Olivia continued sadly, "Magdalena had to go in and give her testimony as well, though I don't think they cared overmuch for the suffering of a lowly house nigger.

"After hearing our stories and the doctor's testimony about the boot print on my chest from Montrose's kick, they called it self-defense and let me come back home," she said with a soft smile on her lips.

"Simon's father is still threatening to take it to higher authorities, but with Simon's long list of past offenses against women of gentle birth, father doesn't think it will go very far up the ladder." She brushed a strand of hair from Devaroe's brow.

"No matter how much money the Montrose family has put into the Democrats' political coffers, none of them will stand up for a known abuser of women whose father has always bought him out of trouble."

"I will testify in your defense," Devaroe said as he squeezed her hand. "I was awake for most of it. He assaulted you, then you allowed him to call off his pack of hounds, and he refused," Devaroe sighed. "No jury in the country would convict a woman in that situation when she has two witnesses, even if one of them is just a Negress."

His comment, referring to her sister, irritated Olivia, and she pulled her hand from his grasp, took the flask, and left the room. "Goodnight, Mr. Devaroe," she said before shutting the door.

This man is driving me insane. One minute he is the sweetest, most charming man in Louisiana, then he opens his mouth, and I simply want to thrash him.

Olivia went to her room, undressed, and crawled into her bed. Magdalena slept soundly, and that made Olivia happy. The past two nights had been filled with fits of weeping, thrashing in the sheets, and cursing.

Olivia closed her eyes, and in what seemed like only a few minutes, strong hands on her shoulders woke her. She gasped in frightened surprise, but Devaroe whispered a hush in her ear.

"Quiet," he breathed. "I can stay away from your

bed no longer, wife." He nudged Olivia over and scooted in beside her, kissing her neck all the time. He ran his hand up and down her naked body and gasped in pain a few times when he moved closer to her.

A hand came over to caress her breast, pinching the nipple into a hard, throbbing button of flesh. His hand went down and kneaded her backside before finding its way between her thighs and exploring her wet, throbbing center.

Why can I deny this man nothing?

"Get back to *your* bed," Olivia scolded in a whisper but shivered under his hot, strong touch and ached for more. "You're in no condition to be taxing yourself in my bed." She reached a hand behind her and touched the hot skin of his hard-muscled thigh, raising goose flesh on his skin too.

"I'll never be in too bad a condition to ignore this," Devaroe breathed into her ear from behind her. "You are irresistible, my beautiful Olivia."

He pulled Olivia's body closer into him, and his hard cock rubbed against her behind. It found its way into the crack and slowly pushed into her.

I will never understand this fascination he has with my behind. It's unnatural.

Devaroe sighed heavily when the meaty head pushed inside her. Olivia did her best not to flinch or squeal, though she wanted to.

First, she did not want to excite him into something more, and she especially didn't want to wake Magdalena and make her think she was being attacked again. Devaroe might find himself missing some very vital parts of his anatomy should that happen.

Soon he pulled out of her ass and found her moist cunny. "I just wanted to get a little taste of that," he whispered to her softly as he entered her hot, waiting cunny. He pushed it in slowly so she could feel every inch of his girth, stretching her open and brushing her throbbing pleasure knot.

"If you insist on continually seeking your pleasure there," she whispered with a quiet giggle, "you will never get me with child."

"Quiet, woman," he chided as he thrust in and out of her with a slow, steady rhythm, bringing on shivers of pleasure Olivia could not deny. He excited her wet cunny until she could stand it no longer and began meeting his slow thrusts with those of her own.

This pirate excites something in me William never did.

Olivia clenched the muscles of her womanhood around his thick, throbbing cock, and he groaned with pleasure. His thrusts quickened, and he panted heavily into her ear. Olivia's explosion of pleasure came with his, and they both tried to stifle their groans without much luck. They craned their necks around to see Magdalena sitting up in her bed with her lips pursed and an eyebrow cocked.

"Miss Livvy, your Mammy, put me in here to protect your virtue against this riverboat man, and here you are ruttin' with him like a damned bitch in heat." She plopped back down on her pillows and pulled the sheet up over her head with a loud sigh of exasperation.

"Does this mean the wedding is back on, Mr. Devaroe?" Olivia whispered as she rolled flat on her back to look up into his ruggedly handsome face.

"Keep wearing that orange blossom perfume and plying me with bourbon, Mrs. Montgomery, and I will take you to Paris and marry you in *Le Notre Dame.*"

"Oh, good Lord," they heard Magdalena mutter from beneath her sheet.

"Very well, ladies," Devaroe said as he slipped out of Olivia's bed. "I will bid you both a very good night," he said and let himself out the door and into the dark hall, buck naked and tightly clutching at his bruised ribs.

"It sounds like he fucks nice," Magdalena quipped as she pulled the sheet back down off her head.

"Yes, that he does," Olivia sighed and rolled to face her sister, who was now sitting up and staring at Olivia. "When he takes his time and gives me a chance to get my pleasure as well, it is *very* nice."

"Yeah, it's nice when they take it slow and easy. When I was fuckin' Jimbo," Magdalena said casually, "he took it slow like that and made me shiver like I was naked in the winter cold."

She was quiet for a minute, and Olivia saw her smile fade again. "Not like those bastards on the road…" She did not finish but rolled over and began to sob into her pillows. Olivia got out of her bed and crawled in next to Magdalena. She wrapped an arm over her sister's quaking body and rested her cheek on Magdalena's shoulder.

"I'm so sorry, Magda," Olivia wept. "We shouldn't have done that here with you in the room. I just can't resist that man's touch."

"It's alright, Livvy." Magdalena rolled onto her back to look up at her sister. "I love you, sister, and I think this riverboat man makes you happy."

Magdalena reached out to take her sister's hand. "It's time for you to be happy again, Livvy. Mr. William's been gone a long time now." She raised her arm and touched Olivia's porcelain cheek with her latte-colored hand. "You should marry that riverboat man and be happy again." Tears trickled down Magdalena's cheeks, and Olivia brushed them away.

"You should be happy too, Magda. We will take you away from here with us and live in New Orleans. You can find a good man there." They fell asleep together, embracing one another the way they had as children, and woke the next morning tangled in the sheets and laughing.

❧ II ❧

The wedding of Olivia Thibodeaux to James Eduard Devaroe promised to be the social event of the year in the Parish with everybody who was anybody invited to attend, except the Montrose family, of course.

On the day of her wedding, Olivia sat in her room being attended to by Magdalena, who fussed with her hair, continually readjusting the tiara affixed to a white lace veil for the occasion. Olivia stood staring at herself in the tall oval mirror in the door of her wardrobe.

"This dress is almost the color of my eyes, isn't it," she said as she held up a bit of fabric from the Josephine dress and ran her hand over the skirt delicately.

"I told you it was the first time I saw it," Magdalena said and stepped back, admiring her work in the mirror from behind her sister. "That riverboat man is gettin' the most beautiful woman in the entire Bayou." They heard the orchestra begin to play, and Olivia rose on wobbling legs.

"Girl," Magdalena chided, "just take a deep breath and calm yourself down. Why you so nervous? You've done this gettin' married thing before with Mr. William."

"Oh, I know," Olivia said and slapped Magdalena's hand away. "But not to him." She gathered up the swishing chiffon skirt and felt the long lace veil trailing behind her. She could feel the weight of the fabric pulling the tiara tight against her hair, wrapped in a tight bun on the top of her head. The lace draped over her shoulders, and Olivia felt like a princess in one of the storybooks from her childhood.

Stepping with grace and care, Olivia walked out of her room and down the flower-festooned staircase. In a formal black waistcoat and top hat, her father stood at the bottom, waiting for her. Olivia thought she saw a hint of pride in the eyes above his scarred cheek as he smiled up at her.

Olivia took his arm, and they walked together through the parlor and out across the patio to a large white canvas canopy erected for the occasion. All the backwater gentry sat in wooden folding chairs on either side of an aisle scattered with rose petals cut from the same flower garden as those in her bouquet. Olivia wondered if her mother had cried at sacrificing so many of her precious blooms for this occasion. When Olivia saw the glow on Marie Thibodeaux's cheeks as she walked down the aisle, Olivia knew her mother had not.

Armand Thibodeaux left her at the side of James Devaroe with a quick kiss on her cheek and took a seat next to his smiling wife, who sat awash in pink silk. *Pere* Dominic from the church in St. Johns stood before them in his priestly robes, sweating, no doubt, in the July heat. The day before had been cloudy, and everyone had feared rain, but the morning had dawned clear and bright. He performed the shortest version of the marriage mass as he could and proudly introduced the new Mr. and Mrs. James Eduard Devaroe to the cheering onlookers beneath the canvass canopy.

Olivia suspected they cheered more for the ending of the long service than the beginning of the lives of the newlywed couple. During the ceremony, servants had set up tables on the patio with bowls of punch and silver trays of finger foods. Inside the house, more tables held trays of delicacies, both sweet and savory.

James, still sore from his pummeling, wore a black silk waistcoat, trousers, and top hat. He kissed his bride at the altar and walked with her hand in hand down the aisle and out onto the green lawn. Magdalena and her mother, Georgia, and the other Negro staff stood outside the canopy's shade to listen to the ceremony and cheered them as they came out onto the lawn.

Olivia, going against all the conventions of the day, broke free of her new husband and went to the crowd of servants and hugged Magdalena, Georgia, and even Jimbo. She considered most of those people who worked on Sweet Rewards her family as much as her mother and father.

Georgia had mothered her more physically than Marie ever had, and Jimbo, who'd taught her how to ride and forage for wild berries in the swamp, was like an older brother to her more than Armand Thibodeaux had ever been fatherly.

Olivia did not care what any of the backwater gentry trash thought about her kissing a Negro in their presence. She ignored the astonished gasps from some in the crowd and continued to hug and kiss others of the household staff, just to amuse herself and Magdalena, who stood with a huge smile as she shook her head when she too heard the gasps.

When she returned to her husband's side, one of the stewards rushed forward with a bowl of water and a rag, expecting her to clean the Negro off her face and hands before joining the clean, white guests at the party.

"Thank you, but I am perfectly clean, Jacob. You can take that away." She held out her hand to her husband, and he took it without reservation.

"That little stunt may cost you," he whispered to her with a laugh.

"Do you think I give a good God damn what this bunch of backwater cane kings think about me?" She laughed and leaned her head on his broad shoulder as they walked into the cooler shade of the big brick plantation house.

Her mother came up and unpinned the tiara and veil so that Olivia could move around the room with ease. "I am so very proud of you, *ma Cherie.*" She kissed her daughter on the cheeks and hands.

Many in the receiving line refused to shake Olivia's hand or accept a kiss. Olivia just smiled as they passed with their noses in the air and made a note in her mind of each one who snubbed her. None of them mattered to her in the least, but someday *she* would be running Sweet Rewards, and when that time came, Olivia Thibodeaux Montgomery Devaroe would remember those snubs.

As the afternoon passed, Olivia, tipsy from champagne and full of shrimp, thought about retiring to her room for a short rest but knew that would not be proper. She did not want to embarrass her parents, so she continued to mingle and chat about meaningless courtships and the problems of grubs or snails in the flowerbeds.

Just after the clock in the hall chimed four, there was a loud pounding at the door, and one of the stewards answered it and admitted Sterling Montrose into the gathering. Olivia heard shocked gasps as the tall white-haired man in his mid-sixties entered the parlor carrying a small, wrapped package.

"Hello, Sterling," Armand Thibodeaux greeted the unexpected guest.

"Hello, Armand," the man said, slurring his words from too much drink. "I have a wedding gift for your murdering, nigger-loving bitch of a daughter." He threw the package at Olivia, who stood nearby. She looked on in astonishment at the white-headed man dressed in a white linen suit fit for the celebration. "Go on, open it up," he demanded without moving from where he stood at the entry to the festively decorated parlor.

Olivia bent and picked up the package carefully wrapped in silver and gold foil paper. She pulled the ribbon on the bow holding the wrapping on, and found a small wooden box. Olivia opened the hinged lid with trembling hands to see two bits of contorted metal lying on a bed of cotton. She peered up at Sterling Montrose in confusion.

"Those are the two slugs they dug out of my Simon's gut," he said angrily, clenching his fists. "I thought you might like them as a reminder of his murder. I don't know what my boy ever saw in you, bitch, but you bewitched him and then refused his hand repeatedly before you killed him."

He took several steps toward Olivia, and both Armand and James moved to block his path. "You can't protect the witch forever, Armand. I have influential friends in New Orleans. I even have more influential friends in Washington. If it's the last thing I do in this life, I'll see the little nigger-loving whore hanged for murdering my sweet boy."

Sterling Montrose, red-faced and ranting, took two more steps toward Olivia. He abruptly stopped, however, and grabbed at his chest. Montrose took a strangled breath, clawed at his pale face, and then fell to the floor. He reached out a clawed hand toward Olivia before he took his final gasping breath with an accusing finger pointing at Olivia.

The silent room broke into an immediate buzz, and those who heard the commotion from outside came crowding into the parlor as the doctor bent over Sterling Montrose and pressed fingers on his neck. He stood and shook his head, indicating the man on the floor had passed from this life.

Olivia, still clutching the little box, buried her face into James Devaroe's chest before swooning into his arms.

Olivia woke in her bed with her mother bathing her forehead with cool water. She felt sick to her stomach and thought for a brief moment that she might vomit. She tried to sit up, but her mother held her shoulder down.

"Stay put, *Cherie. Y*ou have been through a terrible ordeal." Marie wrung the rag in the washbasin and returned to sit on the edge of Olivia's bed.

"I cannot believe the nerve of that foul man to come here like that on your wedding day with such an awful thing and call it a wedding gift. Then he up and dies in the middle of the festivities. We didn't even get to cut your beautiful cake."

Her mother continued dabbing Olivia's forehead, but with every sentence, the dabbing became more like pounding until Olivia finally reached up and took her mother's hand to still it.

"Mother, I am fine." She sat up and realized she

no longer wore the Josephine dress, and that darkness had fallen outside her window. "What time is it? Has everybody gone?"

"Yes, *ma Cherie*, your wedding day has been ruined by that horrid Sterling Montrose and his monstrous gift. Everyone fled in terror after you fainted, fearing Sterling had cursed the entire gathering."

Tears slid down Marie's face at the destruction of the beautiful wedding she and Georgia had worked so hard to put together. "Even *Pere* Dominic fled, crossing himself and muttering prayers against demons. I have never felt so insulted in my life. None of them even cared enough to ask about your condition. Your husband carried you up here and helped Magdalena undress you. By the time he came back downstairs, they all had fled, even the damned doctor," Marie said, shaking her beautifully coifed head. "*Mon Deux*, such a bunch of superstitious fools out here."

"Mother, they are just a lot of backwater swamp rats who've been hearing Voodoo stories since they were children. It makes no difference to me. I am still married. The ceremony was over, and the fools all ate and drank themselves full before Montrose showed up." Olivia wrapped her arms around her mother and kissed her cheek. "It was a beautiful wedding, *ma mere*. I could have wished for nothing better."

Olivia swung her feet out of bed, stood, and wrapped herself in her dressing gown. "Let's go downstairs and cut that cake. I am hungry." Olivia gazed around the darkened room. "Where is James?"

Marie broke into wracking sobs once more. "He is gone, Olivia."

"What?" Olivia gasped, stunned by her mother's announcement. "What do you mean he's gone?"

"I suppose he too was frightened by what happened. He just came back down the stairs, spoke with Armand for a moment, handed him his wedding ring, and left the house. I heard him riding away sometime later." Tears slid down her mother's pale cheeks, and her thin hands shook in her lap, still holding the wet cloth.

Olivia then saw the gold band resting on her bedside table. Shocked and confused, Olivia put an arm around her mother's trembling shoulders and lifted her to her feet. "I'm still hungry," she whispered to her sobbing mother. "Let's go have some damned cake."

❦ 1 2 ❦

Marie took to her bed for three days after the wedding fiasco. That gave Olivia time to get all the reminders of it cleared from the house and grounds. The men took down the canopy, folded the chairs, and returned them to the place from which Marie had rented them.

All the food leftover was sent home with the staff or sent out to the tenant farmers' homes on Sweet Rewards. None of it would go to waste. Olivia took the floral garlands and bouquets down to the cemetery to decorate the graves of soldiers who'd been killed and didn't have family nearby. Her wedding bouquet, she took to William's grave on the property, where she cried and begged him for his forgiveness.

"I promise you, my love, I will never think to love another man. Perhaps this was God's way of telling me that you are my one and only husband."

Tears streamed down her face as Olivia walked from the family plot at the rear of the lawn behind Sweet Rewards. A priest had blessed the tiny fenced area decades ago to make it consecrated ground where the family could be buried.

A large mausoleum stood out there, built by some

long-dead grandparent, but they had put William in the ground. In a letter to her after he went off to fight, William asked to be buried in the earth like his many comrades. He did not want it said that he thought he was better than the soldiers serving under him by being laid to rest in a clean, dry building while they moldered away in the cold, damp ground.

William's family wanted his body sent back to Virginia to rest in their family crypt. Still, the Army had sent it back to Sweet Rewards, as William had directed in his military paperwork. Olivia received several angry letters from his parents and even one from a lawyer who said the family had filed suit to have his body dug up and sent back to Virginia. Nothing ever came of it, and William rested here on Sweet Rewards, where she planned to rest next to him someday.

When all the telltale signs of a wedding ever having taken place at Sweet Rewards were removed, Olivia went into her mother's room to try and lure her out of her bed.

"Good morning, *ma mere*, it is a beautiful cool morning. You should come breakfast with me on the patio while it is still nice."

"I am not well, daughter, just leave me be," Marie said, propped up on pillows in her thin, sweat-soaked cotton dressing gown.

"Mother, you need to come out of this stifling room and get some fresh air. Georgia says, you have not eaten. Join me for breakfast, even if it is nothing more than tea and a roll. Georgia has made some of those lovely cinnamon rolls you adore."

"Olivia," her mother sighed and held out a pale, frail hand. "I have not been well for some time now. I saw the doctor, and he tells me I have a cancer in my womb." Olivia's knees went weak, and she collapsed on the bed, gripping her mother's pale, trembling hand.

"Why didn't you tell me?"

"*Ma Cherie*, there is nothing to be done for this ailment. The good doctor has given me laudanum for the pain, but I have taken it infrequently. In these past weeks, however, I find myself turning to it much more often." She gripped Olivia's hand. "It is why I gave you the bankbook and the key to the townhouse. I do not want you to see me in my decline. I would like you to go to New Orleans. Forget about making an heir to this God-forsaken place and make a happy life for yourself. You are the heir to Sweet Rewards, and if your father cannot deal with that fact, then he can sell the place or burn it to the ground for all I care." Marie fell back on her pillows again. "Your things are still packed, are they not?"

They were. When Devaroe agreed to go ahead with the wedding, Olivia assumed she and Magdalena would be going off with him afterward and left their bags packed except for a few essential things. "Yes, but I don't want to leave you, Mother." Tears began sliding down her cheeks, though she tried her best to stop them. She buried her face in her mother's chest. "What kind of daughter leaves her mother in her time of need?"

Marie put her hands on either side of her daughter's head and lifted it off her chest. "A daughter who obeys her mother's wish that she not watch her suffer and waste away. Go to New Orleans now. You have a place to stay and the means with which to live comfortably.

"I will speak to *Pere* Dominic about having this ridiculous marriage annulled, my sweet girl. Everyone knows the man ran off after the ceremony without consummating it. There will not be any diffi-culty, I'm certain."

Marie reached for a glass of water on her bed-side, and Olivia handed it to her. She took a few halting sips and handed it back. "Go to New Orleans and find a good man who will stand by you, *ma Cherie.* I know I will never see a grandchild," she choked on a sob, "but I will know you are living a life free of this horrible place, a life of parties, cafes, and the opera—a life that I could never live because of your father—and I'll not see you tied to this place be-cause of his desire for a male heir."

Marie fell back on her pillows again and closed her eyes. "I think I will sleep for a while now. You needn't wake me when you go," she whispered before falling asleep.

Olivia picked up the glass of water and sniffed. She recognized the sickly-sweet aroma of laudanum. Marie would sleep for a while without pain.

Olivia sat there for a long while, holding her moth-er's hands and watching her breathe steadily in deep, restful sleep. When she began to snore softly, Olivia smiled. Her father always laughed while accusing her of snoring, but Marie would vehemently deny it. Olivia smiled down at her sleeping mother, aware they all knew she snored regularly and loudly sometimes. She let go of her mother's hand and left the room, closing the door behind her. In the hallway, she met Georgia, who brought her mother a tea tray and a bowl of hot grits.

"She has told you?" Georgia asked, knowing her mother had. She set the tray on a hall table and wrapped her arms around Olivia. "You and my girl need to go now before your Daddy gets back from the fields."

"How long have you known?" Olivia asked the

woman who'd changed her dirty diapers and helped her take her first steps. Georgia was as much a mother to her as the woman she'd just left.

"From the first, when she started having pains and her belly bloated up. I figured what it was and told her to go see that white doctor in St. Johns, but I knowed."

Georgia put a hand on each of Olivia's shoulders. "I been with Miss Marie since we was girls on her daddy's plantation. Like my girl, her daddy was my daddy, too. I will stay with her and see her out of this world, Livvy. I love her just like you love my Magda, and I won't never leave her."

Olivia looked at the woman she now knew was her aunt, as well as the mother of her sister, with wide eyes. "Does Magdalena know that? Does she know she's my cousin as well as my sister?"

"She know. That why you two be so close. She almost close enough to be a true sister." She squeezed Olivia's arms and pulled her close. "Now you and my girl get goin' before your daddy gets back. Jimbo done got Blue all hitched up, and your things is gettin' loaded in the buggy."

She waved a hand when Olivia gave her a questioning look. "I thought it might be today. Magda's got your things packed, and Jimbo is loadin' them in the buggy now." She turned to pick up the tray but gave Olivia a swat on the backside first. "Get yourself goin' now. Your tavelin' clothes be laid out on your bed." Georgia picked up the tray of grits and tea, opened her mother's door, and left Olivia openmouthed in the hall.

The next thing she knew, Magdalena tugged at her sleeve, pulling her toward the stairs. "Come on, Livvy, we got to hurry. Mammy and Miss Marie want us a good ways down the road before Daddy gets home."

She led a silent Olivia up the stairs into her room and helped her change into her red traveling suit. Magdalena wore a long-sleeved day dress and her straw bonnet on her kerchiefed head. She handed Olivia her case that still contained the cash, bank book, and keys. Since their return, it had sat untouched in her wardrobe. She put Olivia's straw bonnet on her head, and Olivia pushed her aside and tied the bow.

"I'm not a child, Magdalena," Olivia fumed. "I can dress myself."

"Well, you are as slow as a pregnant sow," Magdalena said as she led Olivia out of the room and down the wide, marble stairs. They halted in the foyer, and Olivia looked back toward her mother's silent room. "She done said her goodbyes, Livvy. Don't cause her to suffer through it again." Magdalena pulled her through the door and out to the loaded and waiting buggy.

13

Olivia climbed up and took the reins. When Magdalena had seated herself, she urged Blue with a flip of the leather straps, and he took off toward the road at an easy trot. The breeze caused by the moving buggy felt good on the warm morning, but Olivia saw dark clouds to the south and hoped they didn't get caught in a storm before they could get to an inn for the night.

"How long have you known that we have the same grandfather as well as the same father?" Olivia finally asked after sitting quietly for an hour.

"I've knowed for a long time, but Mammy didn't want me to tell it. She said it was for Miss Marie to tell and not me."

"And did you know about my mother being sick too?"

"Mammy said Miss Marie or Daddy would tell you when the time come. It wasn't my place to tell you." Magdalena reached a hand over and put it on Olivia's shoulder.

Olivia wanted to shake it free, but the comfort she felt from her sister's touch made her leave it. "This has been a Hell of a week. I get married, my husband leaves me, I learn my mother is dying, my nurse is my aunt, and my sister is also my cousin. If it weren't so pathetic," Olivia coughed out a laugh, "it would be funny."

"I s'pose when you spell it all out that way, it is kindly awful." Magdalena squeezed her sister's shoulder a little harder. "You can add to it that you're takin' me away from Sweet Rewards just when I an' Jimbo start talkin' about jumpin' the broom."

"I thought you didn't want to marry a cane-field nigger," Olivia said, surprised by her sister's announcement.

"I don't. But to be in the rights about it, Jimbo ain't no cane-field nigger. He's a groom."

"And a damned fine one too," Olivia agreed as she rolled her eyes and smiled. "He could come to the city and get a job in any livery. I'd be more than happy to write him a reference or go in person and vouch for him."

"Jimbo don't want to leave Sweet Rewards. It's his home. His mammy and pappy were both born and buried there. He doesn't know any different and doesn't want to change."

"He's twelve years older than you, anyway, Magda."

"I don't care none about that. Jimbo's sweet and gentle," Magdalena took a long breath and smiled, "and he fuck nice."

"I suppose that *is* important." Olivia laughed, glad the mood had lightened again between them.

"Damned right it is. Jimbo said that if I found myself with a child from that bunch of bastards of Montrose's, he'd be proud to marry up with me and raise my child as his own."

Olivia had not even given thought to the possibility that Magda could be pregnant from their encounter with Montrose's field gang. Then it struck her that she could very well be pregnant with Devaroe's child. At least she had a ring on her finger, for all that was worth.

"If you *are* pregnant, we'll just say your husband got killed in the same accident as mine." The two women looked at one another and broke out laughing.

"Or mine went off with yours on his riverboat and got himself drowned."

That was something Olivia had not considered. Should she change her name to Devaroe or keep Montgomery? The people in the neighboring town-houses knew her as William's wife, but they also knew he'd died in the war. If she started growing a big belly, how would she explain that?

Olivia took a deep breath and let it out. She would cross that bridge when she came to it. Until then, she was Mrs. William Montgomery and would stay that way until matters forced a change.

As they neared the spot in the road where Montrose had stopped them, Magdalena started fidgeting in her seat and brought her knife out onto her lap. Olivia glanced away from the road to see her sister looking around and peering intently into the brush at the sides of the narrow track. She also sat clutching the big knife to her breast with both hands so tightly her knuckles were white.

"I don't think anyone is going to bother us, Magda," Olivia said, lifting the little pistol she had retrieved from her thigh holster as they had neared the Montrose property.

"I sure hope you remembered to reload that damned thing after you unloaded it into Simon Montrose's fat, white belly."

"Mother did as soon as I tried to give it back to

her," Olivia said with a sad smile. "She reloaded it and told me to keep it as a wedding present."

"I bet she never thought your husband would leave you before you ever got a chance to use it on *him*."

"I'm certain she didn't." Olivia snorted a laugh and urged Blue to pick up his pace until they were completely clear of the Montrose holdings. She didn't like the way Magdalena fingered that knife. "Jimbo give you that pig sticker?"

"Yeah, he did," she said with a broad smile and stared off into nowhere, sliding her fingers over the shiny, wide blade. "He told me he'd show me how to use it so long as I promised not to cut his ballocks off with it. He got nice ballocks."

"Really? I heard that the wild Indians in the west cut white men's ballocks off and tan the leather to make gri-gri bags from."

"I bet that'd shrink 'em up some," she said with a mischievous grin, "but Jimbo's would still hold a powerful lot of charm powders."

"How long have you and Jimbo been—" Olivia didn't know quite how to phrase the question. She saw the granite stone denoting the Montrose property's edge and pulled back on the leather reins to slow Blue once more. In the distance, she heard the rumbling of thunder and groaned inwardly.

"How long we been fuckin'? Since the Christmas Party last winter. I drank too much of that Muscatine wine they make out there in the barn, and one thing led to another, and I woke up naked in his bed. I think he was as surprised to wake up with me as I was." She giggled and settled into a more relaxed posture. "We nuzzled a little and decided we liked it and been beddin' together out there now and then. At least when I'm not holed up in your room guarding your precious virtue. For all the good that done." They both laughed until the first light spattering of rain forced them to pull over and put up the top to the buggy. They both lifted the folded leather cover and hooked it in place to keep the worst of the rain off them.

"Jimbo covered our bags with an oilcloth," Magdalena said as she took off her straw bonnet and ran fingers through her black ringlets. "I am sure glad to get that hot bonnet off my head. I'm sweatin' like a whore in Church."

"Me too." Olivia untied the ribbon holding her bonnet, put it on the seat with her sister's, and shook out her long black tresses, letting them fall over her shoulders. The cooler air brought up with the rain felt good on her bare head, and she reveled in it, shaking her hair back as far as she could to allow the breeze to get to her sweaty neck.

The already damp track became a muddy mess, and Olivia had a hard time keeping them in an upright position. The buggy slid and tipped this way and that with Blue doing his best to keep them on solid ground. The rain began falling in heavy sheets, and Olivia could hardly make out the road. Thankful that Blue could see, she gave him the reins and allowed him to plod along at his speed. The wind blew rain into their faces at times, and before long, both of them looked like drenched kittens.

By eleven, they reached the spot where they had found Devaroe the last time they were on this journey. The rain had eased some, but they still slid about on the soupy track. Finally, they turned onto the north and south road to the King's Highway. The wider road made of harder packed earth and red gravel meant the ruts were fewer, and engineers built the road, so it rose in the center, so the water ran off into ditches on the roadside, allowing less standing water. Blue could safely pick up speed, and within an hour, they reached an inn near the King's Highway.

"I think we'll stop here for the night even though it's still early," Olivia told a wet and bedraggled Magdalena.

"Sounds good to me. I think we've stayed here before with Miss Marie on the way to the city. Their cook makes good grits an' greens if I remember rightly."

They turned into the cobbled way to the inn's front, and a groom immediately came for their horse. A boy in a slicker coat came out to ask about their bags, and they told him they would just take in their private cases if he thought their other luggage would be safe and dry in the livery.

"Oh, yes, ma'am, it will be plenty safe. The King's Inn has a good reputation. Ain't no thievin' goes on here." He assisted Olivia out of the buggy while the groom helped Magdalena. They grabbed their bonnets, wrung out their dripping hair, and stowed it up under the concealing straw, ribbons, and frills. Magdalena reknotted her hair and covered it with her white kerchief. Olivia shook out her skirt and straightened her jacket before following the young man to the door and entering the smoky common room of the King's Inn.

Olivia remembered the place as soon as she walked in and smelled the combination of tobacco smoke, stale liquor, and mildew. White-trash sharecroppers, fishermen, and crabbers filled the room. They whiled away a rainy day on cheap alcohol and paid women, a few giving her and Magdalena leering stares and a few crude whistles. Olivia saw Magdalena fingering her knife and gave her a little shake of her head. The one thing they did not need was trouble with the locals.

As they walked up to the fat proprietor's counter, strewn with torn and crumpled pieces of paper, empty plates, and half-full mugs of beer, more people came jumbling through the door. Olivia thought she recognized the woman but could not be certain. When her brood of caterwauling children came bursting through the door behind her, she recognized them as the Pulliers, a shrimping family from the north end of Bayou Tesche. The woman tried to put on airs, bragging about her trips to the opera in St. Martinsville and her grand house. There were some very elegant houses around St. Martinsville, but Emily Pullier's would never come close to any of those.

"We need a room for the night, please," Olivia told the proprietor, raising her voice to be heard over the four boisterous children.

"Yes, ma'am, but your nigger girl there will have to sleep on one of the benches in the common room."

"Excuse me?" Olivia asked, exasperated, tired, and on edge because of the raucous children. "The Thibodeaux's and their retainers have been frequenting this inn for years. My maid will share a room with me."

"I suppose that will be alright," the fat man behind the counter said, eyeing the woman behind her and Magda nervously, "but she has to sleep on the floor using her own bedding."

"Do we look like we have bedding? If you do not have a cot available for her, Magdalena will share my bed," Olivia told him hotly.

From behind them, Olivia heard a surprised gasp and then felt someone push past her to the counter.

Emily Pullier slapped a hand on the wooden counter and cleared her throat loudly. "I hope you are not going to allow this nigger to sleep in a bed and use a chamber pot that decent white women and children will have to use after her." She looked back at Olivia and smirked.

"Well, if they allow filthy shrimper trash to stay here, why would the retainer of a genteel family like the Thibodeauxes be a problem," Olivia returned. "The rotten shrimp stink on this lot is turning my stomach already."

"If you are gonna allow this nigger to sleep in a bed in this establishment, I will be taking my business elsewhere, and everyone is gonna know from me that the King's Inn is nothin' but a filthy nigger-lovin' establishment."

The proprietor looked from the bedraggled woman in an ill-fitting, home-spun dress and her ragged, muddy, snot-nosed children to Olivia and Magda in their wet but well-tailored clothing and said to Olivia, "Your maid is most welcome to share your bed, ma'am. The Thibodeaux family have been good customers of this inn, and *their* patronage is much appreciated."

Olivia edged Emily away from the counter without looking at her. "Thank you, sir. How much will that be, and could we order a meal sent to our room? We need to dry these clothes before coming to eat, and I fear that won't be before morning."

"Yes, ma'am, that will be two dollars for the room and fifty cents each for a tray. The wife has a nice ham, greens, grits, and cornbread if that will be alright."

"That sounds delightful," Olivia told him and opened her case to take out her cash. She unfolded the stack of twenty-five one-dollar notes and handed him three. She returned the bills to her case, clasped it, and waited for the man to get a key from a row of hooks behind him.

When the clerk turned his back, Emily Pullier turned to Olivia with narrowed eyes. "I s'pose you're runnin' off in shame for shootin' poor Simon Montrose, then killin' his daddy at your weddin' to a man who run off from ya as fast as he could."

"I see the swamp-rat gossips have been hard at work," Olivia replied coolly. She took the key and shoved past Emily. "You really should teach these little brats some civility in public. They're an embarrassment."

"How dare you insult my children," Emily snapped and grabbed Olivia's shoulder with rough, red, clawed fingers. "You and your family look down on mine because you live in a big house on a sugar plantation and can buy off the law even after committin' cold-blooded murder." Olivia heard the room behind her quiet as the onlookers listened to the women's exchange.

"I don't look down on you, Emily *Casper* Pullier. Like my peers, I don't look at you at all." Olivia emphasized Emily's maiden name because everyone in the bayou knew her father and brothers spent more time in jail than out for petty crimes. Two of the brothers had spent time in a military prison for desertion during the war. The Caspers were the lowest of the low in the bayou, and though Emily had tried to claw her way up, she would never fit in with the backwater gentry.

Olivia and Magda climbed the stairs to find their room with Emily Pullier screaming profanities at them. When they found the room, they could still hear the woman screaming.

"You most surely pulled on her tail, Miss Livvy."

Magdalena laughed as she shut the door behind them and turned the key to lock it.

"The bitch deserved it." Olivia fell back on the bed and sighed. "It sounds like the story of my beautiful wedding has traveled all around the bayou. Mother was right. It's time for me to go to New Orleans and get the hell out of this swamp."

14

Nothing of merit plagued the rest of their trip into New Orleans, and they arrived at the townhouse on Basin Street well before dark the following afternoon. Olivia parked the buggy in the alley next to the block of four townhouses to unload their bags before taking it to a nearby livery where she could leave it and Blue.

Magdalena undid the oilcloth tarp and pulled it back to reveal their bags open and riffled through.

"Damnit," she exclaimed, and Olivia came hurrying back to see what the problem was. "The thieving sons-of-bitches went through every bag and then just left them open. Weren't nothin' in mine of any account. How 'bout yours, Livvy?"

Olivia looked at the jumbled mess and sighed. "My silver vanity set, but that was all. I had my jewelry in my satchel I took in with me."

"Well, you can sure count on them bein' gone. "I'm going to write Mammy and tell her about this and to spread it that the King's Inn has thieves workin' there. She'll make sure all the families know about it right quick."

Although it had been illegal to educate slaves,

both Georgia and Magdalena had been educated by their respective mistresses in their homes on the plantations. Some tutors flatly refused, but most needed the money and overlooked their young pupils' skin color.

"If we hadn't been wet and hungry, I'd have traveled on past that place, but the next good inn would have been hours away." Olivia began stuffing garments back into the cases and buckling the straps to carry them into the house. Some garments they just draped over their arms to carry around the corner of the building to the front door on the cobbled street side of the townhouse.

Walking back into the townhouse brought back so many memories. Olivia's eyes began to tear as soon as she looked across the room to the French doors leading out to the courtyard. She and William had spent so many happy hours out there reading to one another or sharing meals with the neighbors, cooked over a fire pit in the center. She remembered the laughter and the merriment of those times, and the tears slid down her pale cheeks from her violet eyes to drip onto her jacket.

"Oh, Livvy." Magdalena saw the tears and wrapped an arm around her sister's shoulder. "Don't be thinkin' 'bout the old times. Think about all the new times."

Olivia blinked back the tears, wiped her face with the sleeve of her jacket, and took a deep, cleansing breath. "You're right, Magda." She wiped the dust from the round oak table separating the kitchen from the parlor area. "We need to clean this place up. I don't think anyone's been here since we visited before the workmen finished."

"No, me and Mammy came with Miss Marie last

fall before Christmas to shop. You were off visitin' that friend of yours in Shreveport."

"She was still well then? My mother?" Olivia asked as she started up the stairs to the bedroom.

"Miss Marie just had found out from the doctor. She wanted Christmas to be extra special that year."

A moment of grief and pain struck Olivia. Christmas had been extra special with a huge loblolly pine, cut from one of the forested areas north of Sweet Rewards. Georgia, Magda, and Marie had festooned the stairway and mantle with garlands and bright red potted poinsettias brought up from the Islands. Georgia had baked her delicious fruit cakes, and she had hung the tree with cookies decorated with colored sugar and frosting. Gifts wrapped in brightly colored foil paper and tied with marvelous bows piled around the tree for everyone, including the stables' household staff and grooms. Marie had included everyone in the festivities. War widows and orphans filled the house for a huge dinner of goose, turkey, and ham with all the fixings.

Olivia could not remember a grander Christmas at Sweet Rewards. It would be one she would remember for the rest of her life. Her mother had certainly thought it would be her last with the family and went all out to make it a festive and memorable occasion.

Olivia remembered her father griping about the cost of it all, but her mother, to Olivia's dismay, had told him to hold his tongue and enjoy the season. In most cases, Armand Thibodeaux would have slapped his sassing wife, but he had not. Olivia smiled, remembering him dressing up as Father Christmas to hand out stockings to the children and baskets of food to the widows before the big dinner. He kept on the costume, complete with the white beard covering his scar so the children would not be frightened.

Glancing back down at the townhouse's parlor, she remembered Christmases with William there, and tears stung her eyes once more. Here she was back in their home without him, and the thought saddened her so.

She trudged up the stairs to their bedroom, complete with a privy closet. The smaller bedroom, where Magdalena would sleep, only had a chamber pot, but it had a full bed, a nice wardrobe, and a vanity with a mirror. Olivia made certain her sister lacked none of the finer things living in a townhouse had to offer. Most servants found themselves relegated to the attic, but Magdalena was no true servant.

All the neighbors knew of her parentage. Some scoffed at Olivia's treatment of a lowly Negress servant and would not suffer her being included in the joint dinners shared in the courtyard. Magdalena hosted a dinner inside for the maids and house girls of the other townhouses on those occasions.

Olivia would have to go around and meet the new neighbors. Since the war, many of the tenants had changed. She was not sure who still lived in the other houses. When she and William had lived there and her grandparents before that, this had been a relatively good address, but since the war, the city had shifted, and people in New Orleans no longer held the townhouses on Basin Street in high esteem. Taverns had replaced cafes and exclusive boutiques with more common shops. The neighborhood housed more of the mundane working-class people of the city than before the war.

This shift did not bother Olivia in the least. Knowing that few of the backwater gentry would be present on the streets here suited her just fine. She could live her life as she chose without rumors filtering back home, causing her parents grief.

Olivia threw her suitcases on the bed and draped the loose dresses over a chair to be hung in her wardrobe later. Dust covered the vanity in a thin layer, giving the oak top a white, powdery finish. Tomorrow she and Magdalena would give the place a good cleaning and take stock of what they would need from the mercantile and the green-grocer. Two streets over, the open-air market where farmers and fishermen sold their goods was always a delight to wander.

"This place nothin' but dust and cobwebs." Magdalena came in and opened up the French doors leading out to the balcony over the street. "I thought Miss Marie paid someone to come in and keep this place clean in case the family popped in unexpectedly."

"I think she does, but Benjamin and his wife are getting up there in years." Olivia shook the dust from the lace curtains on the doors, creating a powdery storm in the room. "I think their son just comes around now and then to make sure people know the place is looked after and won't try to break in." She pulled the cotton cover off the bed and shook it out over the street. Olivia breathed in the fresh, salt-laden air of the nearby Gulf and smiled. Sea birds squawked in the sky above, and in the distance, she could see the masts of the tall ships in the harbor. For a moment, she wondered if any of those ships belonged to James Devaroe. She left the doors wide open to air out the stale room, though the threat of mosquitos still loomed here. If a few of the little buzzing beasts got in, she would deal with them later. For now, she wanted the fresh air and what was left of the daylight to put her things away.

"Did you open your doors, Magda?" Olivia asked about the French doors in her sister's room to the balcony over the courtyard.

"Yes, ma'am, Miss Livvy, ma'am, and I opened the ones downstairs too, ma'am if you was wonderin'."

Olivia rolled her eyes and laughed to herself at her sister as she pounded the dust from the pillows on the bed and shook out the doilies from the bed-side tables. "Hello, Miss," someone called up to her from the street. "I'm Ben Benoit. Me and my folks look after this place. Are you with the Thibodeauxes?"

"Hello, Ben," Olivia called back to the tall young man with curly blonde hair and a sunburned face, "don't you recognize me? It's Olivia." She and Ben had played together as children. Three years older than her and a head taller, he had always won their games, but she could always find him when they played hide and seek. The Ben she looked down at now still had the bright blonde hair that gave away his hiding places, but now he towered much more than a head taller than Olivia, and the once skinny, lanky lad had grown into a broad-shouldered, mus-cle-bound man. "I'll be down in a minute," she called to him and threw the now dust-free doilies onto the bed as she rushed out of the room and down the stairs.

Olivia opened the front door and noted it needed a fresh coat of green paint. The light from the setting sun shone on the front of the town-house, and she saw that the entire building could use some attention. The once butter-yellow paint had faded to a dull creamy color, and the paint on the tall green shutters appeared to be peeling, as well.

"Come in," Olivia offered, smiling. Upon a closer look at her childhood friend, she saw his shoulders were exceptionally broad, and Olivia wondered if he could even fit through the door.

The big, blonde man turned sideways and had to duck his head a little to get inside, but he came in and peered around the room as if to make certain everything still sat in its proper place.

"I work at the livery just down the block," he told her without meeting her eyes. "Mama has been ill for the last few months and hasn't been here to dust and sweep. I hope that's not a problem for you, ma'am."

"Don't you ma'am' me, Ben Benoit," she called to the man, grinning, "it was Livvy when we played tag in the courtyard, and it's Livvy now, too. How is your father?"

"Papa died last winter of influenza. I've been lookin' after things since then." He looked around and shuffled his feet nervously in her presence.

"I am so very sorry, Ben." She put a hand on his shoulder, and he flinched a little at her touch.

"And I was sorry to hear about your husband. I was a drummer for the infantry at Vicksburg. The Captain was a good soldier."

"You knew William?" Olivia looked at the man in a different light now. Not only had he participated on the battlefields, but he had known William.

"Yes, ma'—Livvy," he corrected with a shy grin. "He remembered me from here when I came with Papa to do work around the place, and he asked for me to be in his company. I think he thought he had to look out for me because of Papa bein' a Thibodeaux family retainer."

Olivia smiled, knowing that would have been exactly what William would have done. "If you work at the livery, could you take my horse, Blue, and my buggy down there and store it? I'll come down in the morning and make payment to the manager."

Ben puffed up a little, standing taller and squaring his broad shoulders. "I'm the manager of the livery and do the blacksmithing, as well. It's a dollar a week to keep and feed your horse, but keepin' your buggy won't cost nothin'."

"Wonderful." Olivia smiled and opened her bag. She counted out ten dollars and handed it to him. "Here is ten weeks' worth, and I'll come in sometime this week with enough for six months." She walked to the stairs and called up, "Magda, do we have everything out of the buggy now?"

Magdalena came to the top of the stairs and looked down to see Ben standing there. "Is that Ben down there?" she asked and skipped down the stairs. "Good Lord, boy, what your Mammy been feedin' you?" she asked with a big smile.

"Shrimp and rice, mostly," he replied and wrapped his arms around Magdalena, who had also been their playmate as children.

"Well, she must be puttin' some extra special gri-gri in it to grow you up so big from that skinny little boy we chased around the streets with."

Ben smiled and put the money in his pocket. "I don't know what she puts in it, but I've surely been missin' her cookin' since she took to her bed."

"What wrong with Miss Evangeline?" Magda asked as she pulled on the handle for some water from the sink pump for a drink of water.

"She won't go to no doctor, but I think she's just grievin' herself to death over Papa. They were very close, you know," he told them with a sad stare out into the empty courtyard. "Did you see the fountain we put in?" They all walked to the doors and peered out into the courtyard, where an alabaster-white fountain trickled in the late afternoon glow. "Papa found it in a pile of rubbish after one of the big houses was bein' fixed up and thought it would look nice here."

Olivia admired the beautiful piece but felt saddened that the fire pit now no longer existed. The fountain had taken its place in the red-brick courtyard.

"The sound of that water is pretty and all," Magdalena said, "but it gonna have me on the pot all night long."

"Want to trade rooms with me and listen to street noise all night?" Olivia asked, laughing.

"Yes, and that noise is pretty bad now that the tavern has opened down the block," Ben told them with his brows furrowed. "You ladies shouldn't be out too late after dark in this neighborhood. That place draws a scurrilous bunch from the wharves. There's always fights and knifings goin' on there," he told them with his face grim.

"We'll keep that in mind." Olivia went into the small kitchen and looked around. "I'd offer you some coffee or tea, but we just got here and haven't got things organized yet."

"That's alright, Livvy. It's nice to see you and Magda again. I'll be goin' now and get your horse stabled and rubbed down. I imagine he needs it after that long trip in the rain."

"Thank you, Ben," Olivia said, smiling at the man's broad, muscular back as he walked toward the door. "I'll see you soon with the rest of Blue's stabling money."

"No hurry on that, Livvy. I know you're good for it, and I know where to find you." He laughed at her, turned, and ducked out the door, and headed to the alley.

"Now that boy turned into one fine hunk of man-flesh." Magdalena giggled and sipped her water. "I bet he's still sweet on you, too. He couldn't keep his eyes off your chest when you weren't lookin'. You want some water?" Magdalena pumped some more water into her glass and reached for another from the open cabinet. She handed the heavy green glass to Olivia, who took it and drank deeply.

"Thank you, sister, that would be nice. The water from this well has always been so sweet and comes up nice and cool."

"Daddy say this house has a deep well down past the point of bein' salty from the Gulf or dirty from the river."

All four townhouses pumped from the same well, and Olivia could never remember it going dry, even in the driest and hottest of summers, though those were relatively few dry ones here in southern Louisiana.

"I hope all the storm shutters are still working," Olivia said as she shook the dust from the curtains over the French-doors to the courtyard and the one window on the street side of the parlor. That one was wide with multiple panes of heavy wavy glass. It took four panels of the airy lace fabric to cover it. Dust filled the room as she shook them out, and both she and Magdalena began sneezing and rubbing their eyes.

"Will you stop that," Magdalena said before emitting another loud sneeze. "We can take them all down and throw 'em in a washtub tomorrow."

Olivia relented, realizing the futility, and dropped down onto the blue velvet settee. The room began to darken as the sun fell behind the buildings across Basin Street and Magdalena began lighting lamps.

"We gonna need some oil for these lamps, and we better get the kind with the tansy oil in it to keep away these damned, pesky mosquitos."

Olivia went to the desk next to the little fireplace and rummaged in the drawer for some paper and an inkwell that was not dried up. When she finally found one and a sharpened quill, she set to work making a list.

"Look in the canisters and see what we need in the way of dry goods from the mercantile," she told Magdalena, who still rummaged around in the kitchen.

"Oh, sweet Jesus," Magdalena said with her nose wrinkled, "that tin of lard is rancid as Hell. The coffee tin is almost empty, and what is here is most probably stale. It looks like we got plenty of bags of tea, and it been sealed up good." She continued to look in canisters and bins in the small kitchen. "The flour and meal here are both full of weevils, so put them on your list. We gots plenty of sugar, but if you want to make some bread, we gonna need some fresh yeast. We should get some eggs, butter, bacon, ham from the market, and some fresh fruit. If they have some berries and peaches, we can make up some jams and such to put away for winter. It might be good to get some rice and dry peas too."

"If we're going to do preserves, we are going to need crocks with seals or some sealing wax."

"Your crank churn is here in the cabinet," Magda said, lifting the square glass jar with a crank on the top that turned little wooden paddles inside. "We can just get some cream and make our own butter. Freshly made is better than what's been sittin' for God only knows how long at the market."

Olivia agreed and crossed butter off her list, replacing it with cream. She also added a column for the bakery that listed croissants, baguettes, and pastries. Both she and Magdalena were excellent bakers, but why heat the house with baking when she could buy bread and pastries from one of the many excellent bakeries in the area?

"Is that cake plate with the glass lid still here?" Olivia asked as she scribbled.

"Yes, but the base has been chipped some. It will still stand, and the cover is fine. I guess thieves and looters don't care much for kitchen wares." Magdalena laughed. "Most all the basics seem to be here, but the good silver is all gone along with the tea service and trays. They were only pewter, but I guess they couldn't tell the difference if it was polished. I hope you weren't planning any fancy afternoon tea parties, Miss Livvy, ma'am. We still have the pretty porcelain, though," Magdalena teased as she came in and dropped onto the settee.

"I think I'll limit my entertaining to meeting the neighbors to see who is still here and who's gone."

"I hope that crabby old Purdue couple are gone. I never met such a rude, hateful couple in all my days. Their girl, Suzy, said the old man caned her and tried to bed with her regular-like."

"I doubt they're still here." Olivia finished her lists and joined her sister on the settee. "They were both old when we lived here, and that was seven years ago. Some old folks are just set in their ways, and they lived with slaves all their lives. It's hard for them to adjust. Shall we find a café and get some supper? There used to be one up the block and across the street."

"You think we should be goin' out in the dark? Ben said it weren't safe around here no more."

"You have your knife, and I have my pistol." Olivia smiled and patted her thigh. "I feel plenty safe."

"If you say so, Miss Livvy, ma'am. Let's go. I'm powerful hungry." Magdalena giggled as her sister slapped at her shoulder.

15

They left the townhouse with the light of dusk. The street lights along Basin Street had not been lit yet. They crossed the street to bypass the rowdy tavern, and Olivia saw the wrought-iron tables and chairs sitting in front of the café she remembered. They picked up their pace and arrived to find the place still open for business, with waiters lighting candles on the tables and around the overhanging balcony that protected their customers against the weather.

They took seats, and the men lighting the lamps kept giving them sideways glances without speaking to them. One of the men went inside, and soon another gentleman in a waistcoat and string tie came out. He headed straight for them, looking stern.

"Good evening, madam," he said to Olivia, "but I am afraid your girl can't sit out here. If you want to order something for her, she can go fetch it at the kitchen door and eat it standing out back."

"Sir, my family, and our retainers have been patronizing this establishment for decades, and never have our servants been relegated to the back of the building like stray dogs begging for scraps. We were always allowed to eat here as long as we ate out here on the sidewalk tables."

"I am sorry, madam, but with the Black Codes instituted by the state since the war, persons of color are not allowed to eat at the same tables possibly occupied by white customers. Down closer to the waterfront, there are some nigger establishments where she would be welcome."

"Very well, sir, but could I order some food to take back home? We just got here to my townhouse and have not provisioned it as of yet. I thought the Republican administration disavowed all the Black Codes here in Louisiana."

"Most of my customers are Democrats and still abide by the old codes of the proper government, not these Republican Yankees," he sneered, looking at Magdalena. "I believe the cook can wrap something up for you to carry home. I would recommend the rice and peas with shrimp, a nice loaf of bread, and perhaps a chardonnay bottle. But your girl will have to stand in the street to wait. She can't sit at the table."

"Very well," Olivia said curtly. "But *my girl* will wait right here with me. She is not a dog; you can shoo away to the street."

The man went back into the building, and several people looked at them as they came up to the café and went inside rather than taking a table out in the fresh air with them.

"I'm sorry, sister," Olivia sighed as she watched coaches pass on the cobbled street. "I had no idea things had gotten so bad here in the city. I had read that the White League was trying to put Kellogg out of the office for his pro-Negro views, but I couldn't imagine it had gotten so bad."

"It's fine, Miss Livvy," Magdalena said, playing

her part as the resigned servant of a Lady of Class. "Food always taste better at home where we can relax and enjoy it without all these highbrow folks givin' you dirty looks for sittin' out here with your house nigger."

"But this is ridiculous. When you were my property, it was fine for you to sit out here and eat with me, but now that you are free, you must eat at the back door like something dirty?"

"Don't you worry 'bout it none, Miss Livvy. Tomorrow we'll go to the market and get food to cook at home. I guarantee my cookin' be better than anything we be gettin' here or anyplace like it."

"I know that for certain," Olivia said as the man in the waistcoat came out with a short wooden crate containing a chaffing dish, a narrow loaf of bread wrapped in white paper, and a bottle of wine. He sat the box in front of Magdalena without looking at her.

"That will be three dollars, madam because I have to charge you for the dish."

"Of course you do," Olivia said with a huff and handed the man three dollar bills. The man stood there looking at her expectantly for a few minutes while Olivia and Magdalena left their seats.

"Very well, madam," he said with an indignant huff, "come back again soon."

"Not damned likely, and neither will any of the Thibodeuxes from Sweet Rewards or their friends if I have anything to say about it." Olivia joined Magdalena, already a good way up the sidewalk, leaving the man standing at the table open-mouthed.

"Stupid little man," Olivia spat. "Does he honestly think I'd come back to his shabby little café after being treated that way?"

"It the new way in Louisiana, Liv. All the white people are afraid of us niggers now. They think we gonna rise up against our old masters and kill 'em all or somethin'. They all a bunch of fools. This country ain't like the Islands where them niggers run crazy killin' and rapin' when they got free. People ain't like you, sister. They see black skin, and they think we like a bunch of pigs been set free in the field that's gonna run crazy rootin' up and destroyin' everything we see."

"That's just it, sister; you are darker than me but lighter skinned than most of the white folks out there with mixed Indian blood. You have almost as much white blood as I do. The same blood as I do, for God's sake. They should not see you as a black-skinned woman. From now on, when we're out in public, you walk by my side, not behind, and stop talking like a backwater cane-field nigger. You know proper diction, and I want you to use it all the time."

"Livvy, folks aren't ready for educated, well-spoken niggers. It will scare them."

"Let the foolish sons-of-bitches be scared. You are my sister, and these low-born fools will treat you as such. Tomorrow we are going shopping and getting you some clothes that befit the daughter of the Thibodeaux family. Take off that damned kerchief. From now on, you are not just Magdalena, my maid; you are Magdalena Thibodeaux, my very much loved sister."

"Oh, Livvy, you don't have to go doing something like that. If Daddy gets wind of it, he'll be here with blood in his eyes. He'll whip the both of us black and blue."

Olivia patted her thigh and smiled. "Just let the old bastard try."

"You may have gotten past the law for shootin' that ass Simon Montrose, but if you shoot Daddy, the law's gonna come down on you hard."

They were almost at their door when they heard salacious whistling and calls from men coming from the tavern.

"Come on back here, ladies," one of them called after them. "I got something here, especially for you." He saw them headed for the townhouse and whistled louder. "I didn't know new meat moved into the quad. Why don't you let me have a poke as a special new meat sample? If you both fuck and suck me nice, I'll bring you back plenty of customers."

They got to the door, and Olivia unlocked it as quickly as she could, and they both got inside with the man still calling to them with insidious propositions.

"I think our new neighbors may be very different sorts than lived here before," Magdalena said and laughed as she set the box of food on the table.

Olivia looked out the door to the courtyard. Through the open doors of the other townhouses' upstairs balconies, she saw men and women in various stages of dress engaged in several different sexual activities.

"Oh, my." Olivia laughed and pulled the curtains shut. "I can't imagine Mother knew this was going on here."

Magdalena looked thoughtful for a minute. "I never noticed anything when we were here last fall, but we were out most days and weren't out in the courtyard much at night because it was chilly."

"I wonder why Ben didn't mention it this afternoon."

"It's a bit of a delicate subject, and most men don't like to broach it with ladies, Livvy."

Olivia got two plates and two wine glasses from the cabinet before grabbing two forks and the wine corkscrew. Magdalena took the white porcelain chafing dish and the bread out of the box and set them on the table with the wine bottle. When she saw what her sister brought to the table, she went back into the kitchen and pulled a small black ladle from a hook on the wall by the stove.

When they took the top off the oval dish, the room became inundated with the savory shrimp dish's mouthwatering aroma. Steam curled toward the ceiling and filled the room with the smell of file gumbo, green peppers, onions, shrimp, and spices from the Islands.

Magdalena dipped the ladle in and scooped out a healthy portion of the rice, shrimp, and brown peas soaked in the savory sauce. She tore off a hunk of the warm, crusty bread and handed it to her sister. Olivia dipped out of the chafing dish as well and took the bread, tearing off a hunk for herself.

Olivia looked at her beautiful sister and smiled. Before tonight, Magdalena would never have dared serve herself before serving Olivia. Many times they had shared the same table, but Magdalena always deferred to her as her mistress.

"Magda, your hair is wavier than mine but not nearly as coarse as your mother's."

"I know. Mammy always said I had *good* hair." She ran one hand over her head to the bun wound tight at the back of her neck while she stabbed a shrimp from her plate with the other. "This stuff ain't bad."

"From now on, wear your hair the same way I do. I'll give you some pins, and we'll get you some proper bonnets with feathers and frills."

"When we go into those shops, you better introduce me as your cousin instead of your sister. It wouldn't be a lie. I am your cousin from the LaMonte side of the family. My daddy may be a Thibodeaux, but my granddaddy was a LaMonte from Biloxi. Some people around here might know that Armand Thibodeaux only has one daughter—at least only one white one." She laughed and took a drink of the wine Olivia had just poured her.

"Very well," Olivia gave a resigned sigh, "you are my cousin Magdalena LaMonte from the Greenbrier Plantation outside Biloxi, who has come to live with me here in the city in the Thibodeaux/LaMonte Family Townhouse which I inhabited with my husband William before he went off to war and was killed."

"That will suffice. Livvy, do you think I can pass for white? I mean, I do have my Mammy's full lips and round ass."

"The lips we'll rouge up, and these new bustled skirts will take care of your ass."

"I thought I done a good job on my dresses," Magdalena pouted.

"You did, sister, but it is time you had some store-bought clothes of the modern style and not things handed down from before the damned war. Skirts are slimmer now with ribbons and big bows to hide your round ass, and the sleeves are not worn nearly so full now."

They finished their dinner, cleaned up the dishes, drank the wine, and talked late into the night, listening to cackling laughter coming from the other townhouses.

"Your mother is going to be so excited to know we are living in a brothel." Magdalena laughed. "I'm going to bed now. Good night, Olivia Thibodeaux

Montgomery almost Devaroe." She laughed more as she went up the stairs.

"Good night, Miss Magdalena Thibodeaux La-Monte." Olivia blew out the lamp and followed Magdalena up the stairs.

16

July thirty-first, eighteen seventy-four, in New Orleans dawned bright and clear. No one could imagine the devastation on its way. Olivia and Magdalena rose early and began stripping down the townhouse to its bare bones. All the curtains went into tubs of hot water to soak the years of dust out along with the bed linens. The windows got washed with rags soaked in vinegar, the wood polished with bee's wax and walnut oil, the floors swept and mopped, and the hearth and cookstove cleaned of their black ash.

In the afternoon, just after Magdalena took the curtains and bed linens off the line in the courtyard, the wind began to blow, and the first fat drops of rain fell. Thunder sounded out over the Gulf, and when Olivia went out onto the balcony, she saw jagged streaks of lightning over the masts of the tall ships in the harbor.

"I think this is going to be a big storm, Liv." Magdalena dropped Olivia's linens and curtains on her bed. "You think we should close the storm shutters?"

"I don't guess it can hurt." They went out onto the balcony wrapped around the building from Olivia's bedroom overlooking the street, the alley, and ending at Magdalena's overlooking the court-yard. They began closing and latching the tall shutters. First, they closed up the window next to the doors in Olivia's room, then they walked around the corner and closed the shutters on Olivia's other window and the one on the south end of Magdalena's room. After struggling with the latch on Magdalena's window's shutters, they rounded the corner and closed up the final window to Magdalena's room. Their hair dripped, and their clothes hung in a sagging mess before they finished.

While there, they wrestled the shutters over the French doors to Magdalena's room and heard their names called from below. Olivia looked over the fancy iron railing around the balcony to see Ben Benoit, his curly blonde hair hanging straight in the drenching rain. "I'm getting the ground floor windows," he called up to them. "I'll get the ladder so I can close up your doors, Livvy. Now go inside and get dry." They could hardly hear the last through the pounding rain and the wind that had grown stronger by the minute.

Back inside, Olivia hurried to strip out of her wet things and wrap up in her soft cotton dressing gown. She waited for Ben to come to close up the storm shutters on her French doors, but he was taking his time. *Perhaps he's just hoping the rain will let up before climbing the ladder.* In the meantime, the wind blew green leaves that plastered themselves against the glass.

"I told you this was gonna be a bad blow," Magdalena came into the room, wrapping her dripping black curls in a towel. They jumped when a loud blast of thunder followed a flash of lightning that struck the balcony's metal railing across the street. "Let's get the Hell downstairs before we get a bolt of that shit between our eyes," Magdalena said as she grabbed Olivia's cold hand and tugged her toward the steep stairs.

The two sisters ran down the stairs and began lighting lamps and the small hearth in the darkened room. Almost an hour after coming down the stairs, they saw a soaked Ben Benoit carrying a ladder to prop against the balcony and climb up to Olivia's room. They heard the banging of the shutters as Ben shut and latched them tight against the advancing storm.

A light rapping on the door and a bedraggled Ben came in dripping water onto the newly mopped wood. They bundled him in towels and pulled him in front of the small, glowing fireplace. Olivia had started a fire to warm both women, who still shivered from their drenching.

Olivia used a towel to soak up the water on his head until his curls returned. "Why don't you take off that shirt," Olivia said, "so we can wring it out and dry it here at the fire."

With some reluctance, he finally began unbuttoning the wet cotton shirt, peeled it off his soaked torso, and handed it to her.

"I ain't takin' off my drawers," he blurted with his cheeks turning red, "so don't even ask."

"Then stand in front of the fire and let it dry them a little," Magdalena told him as she draped another towel over his broad, muscled shoulders, lingering there just a little longer than she needed to fix the towel in place. "You had better take off those boots so they can dry too," she ordered.

Ben did as she told him and removed his wet boots. He handed them to Magdalena, and she set them on the bricks in front of the fire to absorb the heat and dry. Ben rolled off his wet socks and laid them over the top of the boots. Magdalena used another towel to begin soaking up water from his pants by pressing a towel onto his legs and backside. She handed the towel to him to press on the front. He turned away from the women and proceeded to tamp the towel over his groin and the insides of his legs just below his crotch, which Magdalena had avoided in her attempt to soak the water from the fabric.

Olivia took his shirt, wrung out in the sink, and hung it from the mantel. She secured it by the wide collar with heavy marble statues of David and Venus.

"What took you so long with the ladder?" Olivia asked him and handed him a hot cup of coffee boiled from the stale beans in the canister but brewed well, nonetheless.

"I was helpin' the girls in the other townhouses close up the shutters on their places," he replied without giving any sign of embarrassment.

"About that." Olivia took a deep breath. "When did these townhouses become brothels, and why didn't somebody let us know?"

"After the war, Pierre Matisse, who owns that tavern down the way, bought up the other townhouses. I'm certain he tried to buy this one too, but your mother wouldn't part with it."

"Maybe she would have," Magdalena intoned from the settee, "if she knew what he meant to do with the others. Your parents should have let her know about it. Miss Marie would be disgraced to know prostitutes plied their trade around her family's lovely townhouse for all eyes to see." She stood indignantly and strode off to the kitchen to boil water for tea.

"I'm sorry, Livvy. I thought y'all already knew what was goin' on here. Your mother has been back here several times when she was in town." He turned again to face the fire, and Olivia saw tendrils of steam wafting from the backside of his pants.

"I'm certain she has no idea about what is going on here," Olivia snapped, "or she wouldn't have signed the place over to me to have as a residence in town." Olivia watched him pulling the legs of his pants away from his skin as the fire warmed them past being bearable.

"You two plan to stay here, then?" He turned back to face her with a nervous smile stretched across his boyishly handsome face. "That's wonderful."

Olivia saw him glancing at Magdalena in the kitchen. He grinned as he watched her work. She remembered Ben and Magdalena being especially close when they were children, sharing treats and toys. The fact that Magdalena's mother was a Negress never seemed to bother Ben. That was one thing Olivia had always liked about him. Other children in the quadrangle of townhouses would not play with Magda because of her skin color and her station as a servant's daughter. Still, Ben never treated her any differently than he did any of the other children. Once, he even got into a scuffle with one of the other boys for calling Magdalena 'a dirty little nigger.'

Lighting struck again nearby, and Olivia dropped her teacup when the loud crack of thunder followed. The cup was empty, and it landed on her lap, so it did no harm to her dressing gown.

"Shouldn't you be at home closing up the house

for your mother against this storm?" Magdalena asked him as she brought in the teapot to refill Olivia's empty cup.

"We don't have the house anymore," he told them with a sad countenance. "After Papa died, Mama couldn't bear to live there any longer, so we sold it. She moved in with her sister, who has a big house in the District. I live over the office at the livery."

"I'm so sorry," Magda told him and offered to refill his empty cup with tea. When he wrinkled his nose in displeasure at the offered tea, she took his cup into the kitchen and refilled it with coffee. "And you've never married?" she asked when she returned with the cup of bitter, black coffee.

"No," Ben replied, staring at Magdalena with a raised eyebrow. "Magda, why aren't you talkin' normal like?"

Olivia laughed, and Magdalena replied, "You means, why ain't I talkin' likes a Southern Louisiana house nigger?"

Ben nodded his head uneasily but didn't speak, unsure of what was taking place with his friend. Olivia and Magdalena were both slapping at each other with hilarious laughter, and tears rolled down their cheeks. He stood in front of the fireplace, his face contorted in confusion.

"I'm sorry, Ben." Olivia hiccupped through another fit of laughter and wiped the tears from her cheeks. "You are aware that Magda is my sister?" Ben nodded, and Olivia continued, "Before we left Sweet Rewards, I found out that she is also my cousin."

Ben looked even more confused with a deep furrow in his brow above his nose, and Olivia went on to explain everything to him. She also told him about what happened at the café and her plan to take Magda out, not as her maid but as her cousin Magdalena LaMonte from Biloxi.

Ben appeared to chew on the idea for a few minutes, and the women waited in silence, sipping their tea. "It's not like it is a complete lie," Olivia added. "She *is* my cousin, and her grandfather *was* a LaMonte from the Greenbrier Plantation near Biloxi."

"And if you want to be exacting about it," Magdalena spoke up, "my ma… my mother's name is LaMonte because she was born a LaMonte house slave and given that name on her papers. She is Georgia LaMonte, and since she was never married to my father, my name should be the same as hers, LaMonte, though I think my papers would say Thibodeaux because we were Thibodeaux property by then."

"I think it's a grand idea," he finally said. "I've always thought Magda looked more white than black. The only thing holding her back was bein' a house servant to the Thibodeauxes." Ben walked around the settee and took Magdalena's latte-colored hand, and kissed it softly. "It is a pleasure making your acquaintance, Mademoiselle Magdalena LaMonte, from Biloxi."

She stood and curtsied low. "Why, thank you, sir. I am most certainly pleased to make your gracious acquaintance, sir," she said, and Olivia giggled, but Ben turned his eyes away. Olivia realized then that both of them wore just their dressing gowns. He had turned away because when Magdalena curtsied, a bit of her cleavage was exposed to his eyes.

Such a gentleman.

Olivia tugged on her sister's sleeve and whispered in her ear. Magdalena blushed and pulled her gown tighter over her firm cleavage.

"Magda, why don't we go upstairs and get dressed." They rose with a start when they heard a loud clattering outside in the courtyard. Ben was in the kitchen in a few strides, looking out the small window he'd left unshuttered.

"The wind is blowing the slate tiles off the roof," he told them and jumped when another crashed just outside the window. "This is more than just a regular summer storm." He walked back into the parlor and wrapped both women in his muscular bear arms. "This storm is a damned hurricane."

If you lived on the Gulf, you knew hurricane season began in July. The thought of actually getting caught in one had never occurred to Olivia. "Do you think we are safe here?" she asked Ben.

"This is a sturdy building built of brick that the builders plastered over, and there are taller buildings all around it. You may lose some more tiles, but the windows are shuttered. I think you'll be fine here."

"We may starve to death, though," Magdalena quipped. "There ain't a bit of food in this house. We were supposed to go shopping today but got caught up in our cleaning before the storm started."

"I have food down at my place over the livery. I'll run down there later and bring some back. I'll need to check on the horses anyhow." Ben slipped back into his warm semi-dry shirt and buttoned it while Olivia and Magdalena rushed up the stairs to dress in something more than their flimsy dressing gowns.

Magdalena went to her room while Olivia went to hers. The storm shutters rattled over the windows and the doors, adding to Olivia's already riled nerves. She opened her wardrobe and pulled out a simple day dress, and then she pulled out two others and took them to her sister's room.

"Don't even think about putting on one of those

old dresses, cousin," Olivia said and dropped the three dresses on Magdalena's bed. "My cousin from Biloxi will not be going around in old, worn things like those, not even in the house." Olivia rushed back to her room, buttoning her dress as she walked. She left her sister staring wide-eyed between her wardrobe and the fine dresses tossed across the bed.

When they came back down the stairs, Olivia motioned for Magdalena to sit in one of the chairs around the table and began brushing her thick, wavy hair. She brushed the front locks back and tied them with a ribbon, leaving the bulk to hang in glossy, raven waves down Magdalena's back.

"Now, Ben," Olivia said, pulling her sister, dressed in a lovely blue, brushed-cotton dress in the latest style, trimmed with lace and mother-of-pearl buttons, toward Ben. "Tell me this does not look like a perfectly sophisticated Southern charmer off a Biloxi plantation."

Speechless for a moment, Ben simply stood staring at Magdalena with an open mouth. "You're beautiful, Magda," he finally spit out before opening the door and rushing out into the wind and rain again.

"Oh, my." Olivia giggled. "I do believe you might have a suitor, Miss LaMonte."

"You think so?" Magdalena reached a hand up to feel the hair falling down in the back. A house servant never would be allowed to wear her hair down like that. Olivia watched with a smile as Magdalena turned her head to feel the hair swing free on her back. "I think this is the first time I've ever really felt free, Liv," she said as she ran a hand over her hair. "Working in the house at Sweet Rewards just felt like it did when I was a slave. Nothing changed for Mother and me. Daddy still bedded her and sent

144

men to my room to couple with whenever he wanted to. But now I finally feel free." She swung her hair, and they laughed together in the parlor with the rain beating on the street and tiles crashing in the court-yard outside.

17

The storm raged around them for eighteen hours before it finally blew itself out, moving further inland and away from the city. Ben spent most of that time with Olivia and Magdalena. He brought back a feed sack laden with a bacon slab, some eggs, a loaf of crusty bread, and several apples.

They enjoyed a meal of bacon and French toast covered with apples cooked in sugar and cinnamon. Ben also had a couple of fried eggs, but Magdalena did not mind making them for him in the least. Olivia rolled her eyes at the two staring at one another like besotted school children while the slates from the roof kept clattering around them.

In the end, the storm claimed over a hundred lives, destroyed most of the wood-framed houses along the waterfront, and decimated most of the ships in the harbor. Many of the deaths were those of sailors on those ships. Boats docked upriver from the city on the Mississippi escaped damage, but those docked at the city harbor suffered.

The day after the storm, Ben went up on the roof to make an inspection. The storm had blown nearly a quarter of the slate tiles from the roof. He told them it was a miracle the roof had not leaked. When he checked it, he found the attic rooms dry and secure. They hadn't even lost a window up there.

"Olivia," Magdalena yelled up to her from the kitchen, "we need to get some food in this house. I can't survive on tea and toast much longer."

"Fry up the last of Ben's bacon," Olivia called back. "I don't think any of the businesses will be open today or the open-air market either." Olivia spent the morning rehanging the curtains over the windows, now streaming in bright sunlight since they had opened all the storm shutters. "We can go out tomorrow. I want to walk down to the docks anyway. Ben says it is a real mess down there with ships turned over in the water and roofs torn clean off the buildings."

"You have a morbid fascination with destruction, Livvy." Magdalena climbed the stairs with two cups of hot tea. "Why on earth would you want to see all that wreckage and misery?"

"Some of those ships probably belonged to James Devaroe, and it would do my heart good to see a little of his wreckage and misery."

"I can't fault you none there," Magdalena said with a weak grin, "but people died down there Livvy. Do you think they have all the bodies picked up yet?" Magdalena sat on the edge of the bed while Olivia dropped into a cushioned armchair and picked up her cup of tea from the side table.

"I should imagine, but I don't know about such things. Ben said men organized by the constable's office are searching the wreckage, and the fishermen are pulling the bodies of sailors out of the water. The fire brigades are keeping an eye out for fires in the destroyed homes. If a fire gets loose, the whole city could go up in flames."

"Where is Ben now?" Magdalena asked as she stood staring out the window and enjoying the warm sun on her skin. Olivia noticed a new glow on her sister's face but couldn't decide if it came from the newfound freedom Magdalena felt or the attention Ben paid to her. Olivia had walked in and caught them holding hands last night on the settee.

"I think he's out with the fire brigade or one of the search teams down by the waterfront," Olivia said and sipped her tea. "After checking the attic, he said he had some work to do at the livery. Then he was going to go check on his mother before going down to the waterfront to pitch in."

"He's a good man," Magdalena sighed and sat her empty teacup on the table. "Do you think there's a chance he might be…" She dropped into silence while she ran her fingers through her loose hair.

"I think there is every chance in the world, sister. I've seen the way he looks at you." Olivia stood and picked up both teacups. "The curtains are all done up here. I'm going to go down and hang the ones in the parlor now."

"I already hung the ones over the doors." Magdalena stood and followed Olivia down the steep, narrow stairs. "I didn't want those whores or their clients lookin' in our windows."

They jumped when a quick tapping sounded on one of the panes of glass in the French door. Olivia opened the door to see a pretty young woman in a smart pink day dress standing there with a basket on her arm.

"Hello, I'm Nell Perkins, and I live in the house across the courtyard," she said with a smile that showed dimples on her pretty face. "I know you just moved in and didn't figure you'd had a chance to get to the market yet, so I brought this by." Nell handed over the basket to Olivia. "It's not much, but with the storm and all, I didn't figure you'd be able to get to a market for another day or so. Sarah went out this morning and said all the stores had signs sayin' they'd be closed until further notice. Most are still shuttered up." She sighed. "Don't they think folks are gonna need supplies after a blow like that?"

Olivia took the basket and smelled peaches. The contents, covered with a white cloth, could not be seen, but the basket tugged at her arm with its weight. "Won't you come in?" Olivia opened the door wider to allow the young woman entry. She pushed it closed with her hip and took the basket to the kitchen, where Magdalena stood with a sour look on her face. "Won't you sit down and have tea with us, Nell? My cousin Magda and I were just having some." Olivia elbowed Magdalena, and she went out into the parlor where Nell sat in the plaid brocade wingback chair across from the settee near the fireplace.

Nell stood when Magdalena came into the room and offered her hand to Magdalena, who took it reluctantly. "Nell Perkins," she said, smiling as she grasped Magdalena's hand.

"Magdalena LaMonte," she replied with a curt smile. She took her hand back as quickly as she could and sat on the settee.

"Tea would be lovely, thank you," Nell said to Olivia, who still stood in the kitchen watching the exchange between the other two women. "There are some pastries in the basket if you don't have anything already."

"Lovely," Olivia said and busied herself putting plates, saucers, and the tea service on a tray. She took the towel off the basket and lifted out a pewter plate mounded with sticky, sweet pastries. Olivia added them to the tray and carried them to the low table in front of the settee. "I'm sorry, but we don't have any cream yet."

"Oh, that's no problem. In this heat, who does?" Nell laughed, and Olivia thought the young blonde woman quite lovely. Her blue eyes sparkled with genuine merriment when she laughed, and her lips were naturally pink without rouge.

Olivia poured the tea, and they each took a cup from the tray. The awkwardness of Olivia serving Magdalena showed, and she saw the hint of delight in her sister's eyes at their sudden role reversal. Grinning, she offered Magdalena the plate of pastries. "Something sweet for you, cousin?"

"It most certainly is." She giggled, took the plate, and lifted off a sticky bun before she handed the plate over to Nell.

"No, thank you, just tea for me. I've already had my fill this morning," Nell told them, and Magdalena handed the plate back to Olivia to replace on the tray. "This house has been empty for a long time. Did you just buy it, or did old Matisse finally get the folks who had it to sell and move you, two girls, in?"

Magdalena huffed at the insinuation they were prostitutes, and Olivia laid a hand on her arm to keep Magdalena from saying or doing something inappropriate. "I own this house," Olivia told her calmly. "It has been in my family for three generations now. Our grandfather, Gerard LaMonte, owned it originally and used it when the family was in the city from their home near Biloxi. When he died, it passed to my mother, Marie Thibodeaux." Olivia sipped her tea and could tell none of the names she mentioned had any meaning to the girl. "I lived here with my husband, William Montgomery until the war took him. He went off to fight, and I went back home to stay with my parents. We refurbished it after the destruction wrought by the war and have only used it occasionally when in the city since then."

"And your husband?" Nell asked. "Did he make it through the war? Mine didn't."

"No, the Yankees killed William at Vicksburg. We buried him in the family plot behind my parents' home near St. Johns."

"I'm sorry," Nell said, sitting with the cup and saucer balanced on her knees. "I lost my husband at Bull Run. They told me he's buried there with many others."

"Too many lost," Magdalena chimed in with a bite of pastry in her mouth, "for no good reason that I can see."

"You don't think freeing the Negroes was a good reason to go to war?" Nell asked and picked up her cup.

"How many do you see walkin' around free now?" Magdalena snapped. "Most are still workin' on the same plantations for the same masters and still not getting wages enough to support a family. If the law catches them out on the street without papers, they can throw them in jail and rent them out as indentured servants for no wages at all. That's just legal slavery, in my opinion." Magdalena took a breath, and Olivia tried to motion her to calm down, but she persisted. "All those men and boys died fightin' a war that didn't amount to a pile of shit."

"I'm afraid I have to agree with you on that point, Magdalena," Nell said. "I know other political factors were leading to the war, but the emancipation of the Negroes was the main contributing factor, and they have not been freed at all as far as I can see. The Black Codes keep them from getting jobs or being allowed to gather together in one place. Our husbands died for no good reason at all. Governor Kellogg is doing a good job trying to get rid of the Codes in Louisiana and allowing the Negroes to vote and own property here, but the Democrats don't like it and block his way every chance they get."

"Where did you live before the war, Nell?" Olivia asked.

"We had a little farm outside Shreveport. Nothing big, just enough to keep us fed. Jason taught school at the boys' academy there, and I taught at the girls'."

"You were a school teacher?" Magdalena asked in surprise. "What are you doing down here doin'---" She did not finish her question, cheeks red with embarrassment.

"You mean, why am I a whore now?" Nell asked for her. "It's a long story, but after my husband died in the fighting, his brother moved in and took possession of our farm. As a woman, I couldn't claim ownership if my husband had male relatives who wanted the property." She held her teacup out to Olivia to have it refilled and took a long drink of the warm liquid.

"My brother-in-law told me that if I agreed to share his bed, he'd let me stay on in my own house and cook for him, clean for him, and fuck him," Nell told them with tears in her eyes. "I refused, and he gathered up my clothes and tossed them and me out the door. I picked everything up I could carry and went to the barn, where I turned out all the stock, lit a lantern, and set the place on fire. While he was screamin' and tryin' to put it out with buckets from the trough, I snuck around with my feed sack full of clothes and set the house on fire too. Then I lit out for the main road with nothin' but the clothes on my back, the shoes on my feet, and my paltry sack of belongings." She took another sip of tea and sat demurely in the chair.

"I wasn't going to let that lazy son-of-a-bitch live in my house and take over the farm Jason and I had worked so hard to build up. It wasn't much, but it kept us fed. We built the house and barn with our own hands." She rubbed her trembling hands on her skirt. "None of his kin, who all lived close by, even offered to help us any. My folks were gone by then, and my grandmother couldn't do much, but at least she came out and helped with the cooking while we built the place."

Olivia shared the girl's pain. Losing a husband to the war and then being left in the hands of male relatives who possessed their agendas brought them closer than Olivia could have ever imagined. Granted, Nell's circumstances were much more alarming than hers, but she still felt a kindred spirit in the thin, pretty girl. And judging from the admiration in Magdalena's eyes, she was warming to her as well.

"The only thing better you could have done," Magdalena said, reaching for another pastry, "would have been to burn the house with the son-of-a-bitch in it."

"I thought about that, but his father would have had me hunted down and hanged for it."

"And you had no other family to take you in?" Olivia asked.

"No, Granny was dead by then, and her house burned by the Yankees. I had nobody and nothing but the farm. The school had closed, or I could have roomed there, so I sold my wedding rings and found my way here to New Orleans. There was no work here, and on the streets, I met other women in similar circumstances. They brought me into the trade and showed me the ins and outs of working on the streets and in the cribs." Nell drained her cup and replaced it in the saucer on her knees. "I ended up here last year. The rent is reasonable, and Matisse, who runs us girls here, doesn't take a big cut of our earnings like some pimps in the city."

"How many of you are there here?" Magdalena asked.

"Six," she said, "two in each building. All of us are in the same circumstances. None of us wanted to be whores. The war put us here in Matisse's employ. He wanted your place too so that he could have the whole block, but your mother wouldn't sell." Nell set her cup and saucer back on the tea tray and stood. "I wouldn't be surprised to see him here, tryin' to get you to sell or lease the place to him." She walked to the door. "I need to get going now. Thank you for the tea and the pleasant conversation."

"Oh, no," Magdalena said as she smiled and stood to see Nelle out, "thank you for the basket. I was beginning to worry that we would starve before the stores opened again."

"Yes, thank you for the basket," Olivia said before closing the door. "Stop by anytime." They watched the young woman walk across the court-yard, dipping her hand playfully in the fountain like a child as she walked by.

"She's nice," Magdalena admitted, "for a whore."

"And just how many whores have you known, *cousin*?" Olivia giggled as she picked up the tea tray to carry back to the kitchen.

❧ 18 ❧

Three long days after the storm, most of the stores and other businesses in the city finally reopened, and things began to function as close to normal as could be expected. Bells tolled almost constantly to announce funerals over that time, and Olivia's heart ached every time she heard them.

"Get dressed, Magda," Olivia called from her room, "we are going out. I want to go to the bank, and we need to go to the mercantile and the market. Wear the green dress, you look lovely in it, and I have a bonnet that goes with it you can wear."

This would be their first adventure out introducing Magdalena as her cousin from Biloxi. After their tea with Nell, they had both breathed a sigh of relief that the girl had not doubted their relationship or that Magdalena was anything but another white plantation princess from Southern Mississippi.

Ben, who had visited later that afternoon, had assured them he had no doubts their ruse would work. "Magda, you are whiter than I am after I spend an afternoon in the sun fishing. If you keep yourself shaded, no one will ever remark on the color of your skin except to say it is as soft and sweet as one of these summer peaches." He bit into one of Nell's peaches, letting the sweet, sticky juice run down his chin. Olivia rolled her eyes as Magdalena blushed and batted her big green eyes at Ben from across the room.

Magdalena walked into Olivia's room wearing the mint-green dress with cream piping around the yoke, collar, and cuffs. She wore her hair down except for the front and sides, which she had brushed back and tied with a cream ribbon that matched the piping. Olivia pinned a green velvet French bonnet to her head, cocked a little to one side, and changed its feather to one that matched the ribbon in Magdalena's hair.

"You look stunning, Magda," Olivia gushed. "Here." She handed her a gold ring set with an oval piece of dark green jade. "I always wear this ring with that dress."

Magdalena slipped the ring onto her finger and stared at it for a minute. Then she gazed at her reflection in the mirror over Olivia's bureau. "Is that really me?" Magdalena gasped. "If my mam … mother could see me now, she'd whoop my behind for puttin' on airs, not to mention for puttin' on your nice clothes. Then Daddy would whoop me again for steppin' out of my proper place as Miss Livvy's house nigger."

"Oh, stop that kind of talk," Olivia shushed her. "You are my beloved cousin Magdalena LaMonte from Biloxi. I will hear no more talk about house niggers and the like from you." She picked up her drawstring bag with the leather bank book inside, grabbed Magdalena's gloved hand, and pulled her down the stairs and out onto the sidewalk into the gray, overcast morning. The women walked side-by-side on the wide sidewalk, their bags hanging from one wrist and their parasols on the other.

They passed the tavern that was blissfully quiet in the early morning hours and stopped in front of the livery. "I want to go in and say hello to Blue," Olivia said, "and I'm sure you'd like to go in and say hello to Ben." She winked and giggled as she stepped into the livery door that smelled a mixture of hay, horse dung, leather, and coal smoke from the smithy. They could hear the pinging of a metal hammer on the anvil and knew they would find Ben sweating over his forge in the back of the building.

Bent over his work, he did not notice the two women walk behind him toward the stalls where Ben housed the horses. Olivia found Blue, and he came to her happy to take the apple she offered him and the gentle pat on his muzzle as he chewed the fruit. In the stall next to Blue stood a sway-backed old mule, and Magdalena held out her apple to him. He walked up to her with guarded curiosity but gladly accepted the offered treat.

"Be careful of old Buck," Ben said, causing both women to jump, startled at his voice behind them. "He is old and has a bit of a mean streak. He bites and kicks if he doesn't get his way."

Magdalena smiled and petted the gray muzzle of the old mule as he chewed up the apple. "He's just been overworked and underappreciated."

"That he has," Ben laughed, "and I think he recognizes a kindred soul."

"I beg your pardon." Olivia looked at him indignantly. "Magdalena has never been overworked or underappreciated, not by me, anyhow."

"Well, I don't know about that." Magdalena laughed, joined by Ben.

Olivia gave them both a mock pout and grabbed

Magdalena's arm. "Come now, *cousin*, we must be off to buy you a new wardrobe, as you lost yours in a fire and all." Magdalena waved at Ben with a coy smile and a wink as Olivia pulled her back out onto the sidewalk.

"We have to find this bank first," Olivia told her, fishing out the bank book for the address. "Lafayette Bank, ninety-one Lafayette Street, I think that is this way." She pulled Magdalena along for several streets before giving in and stepping into a café to ask directions. Olivia was going in the right direction, but they still had several blocks to travel west and then a few south to get to the address.

When they found it, the Lafayette Bank left Olivia a little disappointed. The building was old and shabby, needing a new coat of paint. At one time, the brick structure may have been quite stately, but years of wear and neglect showed on the exterior. They made their way up crumbling brick stairs and into a quiet lobby. The chipped marble floor in need of a good polishing did nothing to bolster Olivia's confidence in the place.

At the counter, a skinny man in wire-rimmed spectacles stood slumped over a pile of papers.

"Excuse me, sir," Olivia said politely, "I would like to withdraw some funds from my account." She opened the little book and laid it on the counter.

He glanced up at her with rheumy eyes through his spectacles and then took the book to study. "You are not Mrs. Thibodeaux," he said flatly and held onto the book.

"No, I am her daughter, Olivia Thibodeaux Montgomery, and I believe my name is also on this account. That is what my mother told me when she gave me the account book. She said she and my grandfather, Gerard LaMonte, had been banking here for some time."

At the mention of her grandfather's name, the old man's eyes widened, and he stood a little straighter behind the counter. "Gerard LaMonte was a very good customer, and we opened this account in your and your lovely mother's names though it's not technically legal because Mr. Lamonte was such a good customer and requested it of us. We held the mortgage on his townhouse for some years, and your mother, Marie Thibodeaux, has been a faithful depositor. How is she, by the way? We have not seen her in quite some time."

"She is not well, I'm afraid," Olivia told him. "That is why she has passed the townhouse and this account on to me. My cousin, Magdalena," Olivia pulled her cousin forward, "and I have taken up residence in the townhouse now."

"Of course, of course," he muttered, and his eyes darted between the two women. "I can see Mr. LaMonte on both your faces. He was a handsome man, and you are both handsome young women. How much did you want to withdraw today, Mrs. Montgomery? Your mother has spoken of you often. I was sorry to hear of the loss of your husband."

"Thank you ever so very much," Olivia said sweetly to the old man. "I believe a hundred dollars will do for now. We need to buy provisions for the house and make some repairs due to the storm."

"Nothing major, I hope. I always liked that house. A very fine address indeed there on Basin Street in its day." He fumbled with the drawer below the counter in front of him.

"No, nothing major. We just have to replace a few roof tiles, and the place requires paint. I think we'll have it all done at once before it falls into too much further disrepair." Olivia could not help glancing around the inside of the old building in which she now stood.

"Yes, this old place needs a good bit of work, but the owners no longer feel keeping it up is worth the cost. They are talking about moving the whole operation to a more central location. I've been here for almost forty years. I work down here and live in an apartment upstairs. They tell me I'll be able to keep the apartment as a retirement benefit, but I won't be moving with the bank," he told them with sad, watery eyes.

"Forty years is a long time to devote to an employer," Magdalena said sweetly. "It's time for you to retire and sit on a dock in the sun with a fishing pole."

"I do love to fish," he replied and began peeling bills out of the drawer and laying them on the counter. "I hope you don't mind paper scrip. They don't let us handle gold here any longer."

"Paper will be fine." Olivia smiled.

He counted out the hundred dollars, took the bank book, and made the necessary notations. "I added in the accrued interest since the last time Mrs. Thibodeaux was in, and after your one-hundred-dollar withdrawal, you have a total of two thousand, seven hundred and seventy-five dollars and fifteen cents. Is there anything else I can do for you?"

"I don't believe so, but when will the bank be moving and where?" Olivia asked as she put the money and the bank book back into her bag.

"They are putting it in a building on Decatur Street near the Opera House, but with the storm, I don't know when the actual move will be. Some damage to the scaffolding will require rebuilding before the building's refurbishing can be completed. I will have more news the next time you visit," the old man told them as they walked away.

"*Au revoir, monsieur.*" They smiled and left the building.

"I had no idea Miss Marie had that kind of cash hidden away from Daddy," Magdalena whispered. "You are a rich woman, Livvy."

"I think most of it was left to her by Grandfather, and she's just added a little to it over the years as she could. There was more, but she told Daddy she sold the townhouse and took money out of the account so he'd think it was gone."

"Now I see where you got your sneaky side from." Magdalena laughed.

The rest of the afternoon, they spent in dress shops outfitting Magdalena in the wardrobe befitting a southern Louisiana lady of means. They went into shops and tried on dozens of dresses and suits. Never once were they questioned or given any trouble. They brushed shoulders with New Orleans white elite who would have swooned if they'd known a mulatto woman had just been trying on clothes in the shop. They both had to laugh after coming out of some of the shops run by snooty bigots.

"If the stupid bitches think the black rubs off," Olivia laughed, "all y'all would be white by now."

"And most of y'all would be black, 'cause we been washin' your lily-white asses since you slid out the womb."

At the mercantile, they purchased all the things on Olivia's list and a few other items. One of the things Olivia decided they needed was an icebox. They had one at Sweet Rewards, but her mother had never fitted the townhouse's kitchen with one. Olivia knew there was an icehouse in the city and spent thirty dollars for the insulated wooden cabinet that would hold a block of ice and keep their cream, butter, and eggs from spoiling in the New Orleans heat. She paid a little extra to have it all delivered, and the lady at the counter raised a suspicious eyebrow when Olivia gave her the address. She ignored her and continued to the open-air market that smelled of fresh-ground spices, fruit, and fish.

With the icebox purchase, they could also buy more than a day's supply of shrimp or fish. Olivia haggled with the man for a while but finally talked him into selling her a block of ice for her new icebox along with two pounds of large shrimp, a large, skinned catfish, and two pounds of fresh crayfish. Magdalena made the best etouffee in Louisiana, and Olivia was dying for some. He, too, agreed, for a fee, to deliver their purchases.

They bought spices, rice, dried peas, onions, peppers, potatoes, yams, more peaches, blueberries, and apples. Olivia wanted to make some jams and apple butter to put up for the winter.

"Olivia, with the market here, we don't need to put up our preserves. There are vendors here who sell them."

"Magda, the money in the bank won't last forever, and I have no skills with which to make money. Unless you plan to join Nell and the other women in their trade to earn a living, we will have to be frugal. I spent the money on the icebox so that spoilage wouldn't plague us, but until we can figure out a way to make a little extra money, we can't be too free with our funds."

"I'm sorry, Livvy, you're right. I wasn't thinking." Magdalena, crestfallen, remained silent for the rest of their outing through the market and began picking up the packages as Olivia sat them down. Seeing her newly independent sister going back to her subservient habits saddened Olivia and made her feel guilty.

On the way out of the market, they passed a café, and Olivia led them in without regard to any looks from the proprietor. They took a seat at a corner table and dropped their packages on the floor.

"What may I get for you, ladies?" the waiter asked them.

"Tea and beignets, please," Olivia told him.

"Yes. Mademoiselle," he told her, bowed, and left.

"You see, Magda, we've made it through the day. You are now officially my dearest cousin, Magdalena LaMonte, here from Biloxi after losing your home and family in a fire."

"That might play, for now, Liv, but what happens when we run into someone who knows us? This town and this state ain't that big. We're going to run into somebody sometime who knows Olivia Thibodeaux and her nigger maid."

"Oh, hush." Olivia quieted her with a pat on the hand. "We were all over town today and didn't bump into a soul."

"Yes, but everybody is still cleaning up from the storm. What about the next time? Be just our luck, we run into one of them nigger-haters who'll have me lynched, and you burned out of your house."

The waiter brought them their tea and plates of beignets, dusted with powdered sugar. He left, and they dug into their pastries.

"We shouldn't tarry here long," Olivia said and stirred cream into her hot tea. "The deliveries should start arriving soon."

"Was this just another test to see if I could fit in?" Magdalena jabbed and smiled.

"I'm sorry, Magda. I suppose it was, but I needed to eat something too."

"Mrs. Montgomery?" They jerked their heads up to see an elderly woman leaning on a cane coming toward them. "It is you. My Lord, girl, I hadn't seen you since before the war when you left the town-houses. Mr. Mollier and I moved out two years ago when the neighborhood began to decline."

Now Olivia remembered the woman. She and her husband owned the townhouse where Nell now resided. Olivia remembered her as a notorious busy-body who gossiped about everyone on the block. Her husband, a retired clerk from one of the shipping lines, never mixed with the others and seldom joined them in their festivities in the courtyard, preferring his solitude and books.

"And how is dear Mr. Mollier?" Olivia asked, and the woman took a seat with them without being invited.

"Oh, he is much the same," she huffed. "He still prefers his musty old books to good company or fresh air. I will tell him you asked after him. He will be pleased." She looked at Magdalena, giving her an appraising stare. "And who is this lovely young thing?" she finally asked.

"Mrs. Mollier, I'd like you to meet my cousin, Mademoiselle LaMonte, from Biloxi. She has moved into the townhouse with me since losing her home in a fire."

The old woman took Magdalena's hand in hers. "I am so very sorry to hear that, my dear. You are lucky to have such a loving cousin as Mrs. Mont-gomery to take you in. But dear," she turned her at-tention back to Olivia, "that neighborhood has become overrun with trash and degenerates. I cannot believe your family has kept the place. Your mother is such a gentle and aristocratic woman. I am surprised she didn't get shed of the place long ago. I heard the houses are now all filled with trashy women selling their bodies. How can respectable women like yourselves live amongst such squalor?"

"Really?" Olivia said in feigned surprise. "We just met the young woman living in your old house, and she is quite lovely. Didn't you think so, cousin?"

"Indeed, I did," Magdalena agreed. "She is a war widow who taught at the Academy for Young Ladies in Shreveport until it was closed during the war. She seemed quite refined and very well-spoken."

"Yes, a lovely woman who brought us a basket of provisions after the storm," Olivia told her. "She saved our lives. We had only just arrived the day before and had not been able to get to the market for provisions. We had no food in the house, and all the markets were closed."

"Well," Mrs. Mollier sighed, "Mr. Mollier will be glad to know a decent woman is living in our home. Perhaps what I've heard about the Quad has been exaggerated. You know how some people live to carry tales," she said and gave a nervous laugh.

"Indeed," Magdalena huffed and raised an eyebrow at Olivia. "Shouldn't we be going, cousin? Aren't the things from the mercantile supposed to be delivered this afternoon?" She began gathering her bags from the floor around her chair and stood. "It was a pleasure to meet you, Mrs. Mollier, and please give your dear husband our best." She followed Olivia to the counter, waited for her to settle their bill, and went out onto the street.

"You see," Olivia laughed, "that old bat knew you for years as my maid and didn't even recognize you. This ruse is going to be a breeze."

❧ 19 ❧

For two days after their shopping excursion, Olivia and Magdalena busied themselves with putting the house in order. After much rearranging in the kitchen, the new icebox finally ended up not quite in the kitchen but against the stairway wall in the hall that led to the alley door where they kept the trash bins. That door stayed locked and seldom used due to the offensive odor in the alleyway.

Olivia stood peering at the oak-doored, insulated cabinet from the kitchen center with a finger resting at the corner of her mouth.

"Liv, if you think I am going to help you move that heavy damned icebox again, you be out of your ever-lovin' mind. I've broken my back from pushin' that thing around. It looks fine where it is, and it's close to the door so that we can dump the water out of the drip tray." Magdalena dropped into a chair with a heavy sigh.

"No, the spot is fine. I was just wondering if there was enough sun from the back door for a fern. I think a fern would look nice on top of it."

"You and your plants," Magdalena huffed. "No, ferns need to be in direct light like in front of this big window. Begonias would be good, maybe, or violets. How about a sweet potato? They vine out nice and green and don't take much tendin' to at all."

I suppose you're right." Olivia went to the bin, picked out the scrawniest-looking sweet potato, and laid it on the counter. She found an old mug from the cabinet, filled it with water, put the orange root into it, and set it on the window sill above the sink.

"Shall we walk down to the waterfront?" Olivia asked.

"Whatever for?" Magdalena groaned.

"We need to make arrangements with the ice-house for deliveries, and the icehouse is down by the harbor," Olivia explained as she went to the stairs. "I'm going to wash and change."

Within the hour, they left the townhouse together in lightweight cotton suits, carrying their parasols to ward off the relentless summer sun. Magdalena had covered her face and hands with a cream Olivia purchased from the apothecary. The man had guaranteed it to keep the skin from darkening in the sun and even to lighten it some. She had taken it from her sister and promised to use it but told Olivia she doubted the packaging's claims. Magdalena told her sister it simply felt like lard mixed with some beeswax and coconut oil. It did soften her skin some, so she put it on before going out into the sun, as did Olivia to preserve her porcelain complexion.

As they'd heard, the devastation along the waterfront proved to be terrible. The sisters saw homes and warehouses without roofs or destroyed, and ships lay in the harbor on their sides or washed up onto the beaches with their masts shattered and their keels in the air. Olivia shivered when Magdalena pointed out a bloated corpse bobbing in the surf, as yet unclaimed by any of the boats patrolling the waters.

Funeral bells still tolled daily for the victims, and Olivia hoped this poor soul would soon be recovered and given a proper resting place. She turned her eyes away from the grisly mass in the water and continued along the boardwalk following the seawall. A big warehouse with its pit lined with straw, sawdust, and Spanish moss stood where boats from the north brought down huge cakes of ice to be cut up and sold to southerners for their iceboxes and sweet tea.

The walkway bustled with city dwellers curious to observe the devastation, fishermen were hauling their catches in hand-pushed carts to the market, and families with children trying to find a pleasant spot on the beach to cool off in the blue waters of the Gulf. It wasn't surprising that neither woman saw the man until he was right in front of them.

I can't believe she's here. What am I going to say to her? She has to hate me after I ran out on her the way I did. What can I possibly say?

"Good afternoon, Mrs. Devaroe," he said and stopped Olivia with a big, tanned hand on her shoulder. "Or should I say, Mrs. Montgomery?" James Devaroe asked, giving them both a dark, questioning stare. "My banker told me Mrs. Olivia Montgomery had returned to the city from her parents' plantation, Sweet Rewards, and has resumed residence at the family townhouse along with her beautiful *cousin*, a Miss LaMonte from a plantation near Biloxi."

"Yes, Mr. Devaroe," Olivia said nervously as her eyes darted to those passing around them. "My cousin, Magdalena LaMonte, and I are now residing in the city. If you'd be so kind as to let us pass, we need to visit the icehouse." She tried to push past him, but he would not release her shoulder.

"Why don't you and your *cousin* come and join me over here for a coffee?" He pulled them toward a shabby waterfront café with boards nailed over windows and shutters hanging askew.

With reluctance, both women walked with Devaroe to the establishment and took seats on benches set around tables made from boards nailed atop barrels. The place stank of stale coffee and fish, but they sat on the benches and waited for Devaroe, dressed in a casual brown suit, string tie, and straw hat common to the Islands, to speak. A waiter in a dirty white shirt with sleeves rolled up above his elbows came out of the old brick building. "What can I get for you and your ladies today, Mr. Devaroe, sir?"

"We will all have lattes and a tray of beignets, Paul," Devaroe told the man, who bowed and went back into the building.

"So, wife, have you come down here to gloat over my losses?" he asked, gesturing out at the ruined ships in the harbor. "Thank God I had surety on everything, or this storm would have ruined me."

"I *am* sorry for your losses, James, but I am not your wife. Mother has seen to it that *Pere* Dominic has annulled the ridiculous marriage. You left plenty of witnesses, including the good Father, to your desertion of me on our wedding day. You mortified my parents with your behavior, James. I believe you can forget about any shipping contracts from Sweet Rewards in the future."

Devaroe set his eyes on Magdalena in her fine suit and sneered, "And just how mortified are they going to be when they find out you're trying to pass off your nigger sister as your *white* cousin from Biloxi?"

"Magda *is* my cousin through my grandfather from Biloxi. Her mother and mine are sisters, and her skin is whiter than yours is at the moment," Olivia said and patted Devaroe's very tanned hand.

Paul brought out their coffees, the tray of pastries, and three small plates with dingy, frayed cloth napkins. "Will that be all, sir?" he asked Devaroe, completely ignoring the two women.

"*Oui*, Paul, *merci*." The man retreated into the building to leave them alone once again.

"My banker tells me your quad on Basin Street is nothing but a den of whores now. Is that true? Are my wife and her cousin taking up the oldest profession to make ends meet now? I don't know about your cousin here," he grinned rudely at Magdalena, "but with that tight little cunny and asshole, you could probably make a good living at it. I'd be more than happy to give you some referrals."

"You are insufferable, Mr. Devaroe," Olivia seethed and tried to stand. He grabbed her wrist and tugged her back down roughly.

"You haven't finished your coffee, Mrs. Montgomery." Devaroe had yanked her back down so hard that he pulled her glove from her hand. "I'm not done talking to you yet, Olivia," Devaroe scolded. "When I'm finished, and we've come to an understanding, then you and your lovely sister both may be on your way." He threw the white glove back into Olivia's startled face.

"What sort of understanding," Olivia asked, wary of the man's intent.

I can't believe I'd almost talked myself into thinking this pompous ass had feelings.

"I have plenty of whores I bed regularly here in the city, but you are my wife, and I truly do enjoy those two tight little holes of yours." He smiled and reached out to lay a finger on Olivia's pink mouth. "And I haven't had the opportunity to enjoy this one yet." Olivia snapped at the offending finger with her bared teeth. Devaroe pulled his hand away, laughing,

"You will agree that when I am in town, I will visit your bed whenever I please and use you as I see fit. For that, I will not reveal that you are trying to pass off this negress as a white woman. That, you know, is a grievous offense and could find you both suffering *charivari*. I don't think either of you would look good in tar and feathers," he said and laughed maniacally.

"You're an insufferable bastard, Mr. Devaroe. We should have left you to die by the side of the road like the animal that you are," Olivia hissed at him.

"Now, now, wife, don't give yourself the vapors." He patted her bare hand and lifted her wrist to inhale her orange-blossom-scented oil and shuddered with the memory of her in his arms.

Why can't I just tell her how I feel? She's not my mother. She won't slap me and call me a fool for telling her I love her. She's not Suzette Devaroe. Olivia won't laugh at me and send me away. Why can't I just trust her?

"I will present myself this evening, say around six," Devaroe curtly informed them. "Your cousin will have a supper prepared for us, and then we will adjourn to your boudoir where we will officially consummate our marriage vows." He took a final drink of his coffee and stood. "If I enjoy both the meal and the dessert," he said as he grinned down at Olivia and winked, "I will set up an account with my banker to accommodate your household funds every month. I would like to keep your favors mine exclusively." He walked away, laughing, and Olivia wanted to toss their empty cups at his bobbing head.

"I knew this was gonna blow up in our faces, Livvy," Magdalena muttered. "I think I saw some castor bean plants on our way down here. I'll fix his sorry ass a really fine supper with a few of those ground up in it."

"If anyone is going to poison that sorry bastard," Olivia blurted with angry tears stinging her eyes, "it's going to be me, but castor beans would be a good fix. We'll pluck some on the way home. Make sure you have your gloves on, though. I don't want you getting sick."

"Long as the shell of the bean stays on, you can't get sick from it," Magdalena reminded her. "We still goin' to the icehouse?"

"We may as well since we're already down here by the warehouses." Olivia rose and headed back to the boardwalk. She thought for a minute to ask about the bill, but the man seemed to be well acquainted with Devaroe. He probably had a running tab with the shabby waterfront establishment.

They found the icehouse amongst the maze of warehouses, and Olivia made arrangements for regular deliveries of ice blocks cut to size ascribed to their icebox. She paid the man for a month of deliveries in advance, and they walked back toward home.

At the hedge where the dark green, five-pronged, waxy leaves of the castor bush hung over onto the sidewalk, Magdalena bent and rummaged on the ground. She eventually came up with a handful of the brown·speckled beans of the castor bush. Ground into a powder or boiled, they made a deadly poison for which there was no antidote.

The foul-tasting oil pressed from the fresh beans was used as a medicine by some for stomach ailments, though Olivia thought some women used it as more of a punishment or a threat to their children than an actual healing oil.

"I remember your mother threatening us with that horrible stuff when we were children," Olivia laughed. "If you girls don't settle yourselves down and act like civilized young ladies, I'm gonna get out the castor oil," she mimicked Georgia, and they both laughed.

"Lord knows, I've had my share of it," Magdalena said and wrinkled her nose at the memory of the disgusting-tasting oil. She dropped the handful of dry beans into her jacket pocket, and they walked on.

In front of the livery, Ben swept the sidewalk with a worn straw broom. "Hello, ladies," he said with a broad, cheerful smile. "What have you been up to today?"

"Livvy had to make arrangements at the icehouse," Magdalena told him as Olivia passed by them to go in and say hello to Blue.

"Oh, for the new icebox? Having one of those must be nice." He sighed wistfully in the humid afternoon heat.

"Having cold milk is most definitely a treat, and not having to worry about the butter goin' rancid is nice too," Magdalena admitted. "We even have us some shrimp and crayfish in there. They stay as fresh as when they come out of the water."

"What you gonna do with all that?" Ben teased.

"Well, tonight I'm makin' up some gumbo and rice. I can bring some down if you'd like. Livvy is havin' company for dinner, and I'd just as soon not be around."

"Who's comin'?" he asked, noting her obvious irritation.

"Just a fella who's a friend of Livvy's father. We ran into him on the way down to the icehouse, and he just invited himself to dinner."

"That's very rude," Ben said, continuing to sweep the debris from in front of the livery blown up by the morning's winds.

"He is for certain a rude person, but Livvy thinks her father would want her to oblige the man."

"Is her father still lookin' for a husband for her?" Ben asked with a little laugh.

"Yes, it's one of the reasons we came back here to the city. Livvy was tired of all of Daddy's fancy parties to introduce her to new matrimonial candidates, and she hates it." Magdalena glanced toward the livery and saw Olivia coming out. "I'll see you tonight, Ben, with a big, hot bowl of gumbo and fresh biscuits."

"I'll be here." He smiled and waved at the two women as they walked away.

"What's that about gumbo and biscuits?" Olivia asked.

"It's what I'm makin' for you and your *husband*, and as I do not intend to have that bastard inflicted upon me, I'm taking my dinner to share with Ben," she replied, giddy with anticipation.

"Are you trying to win him over with your skills in the kitchen?" Olivia laughed.

"Maybe, but if you and your Mr. Devaroe are going to be making a night of it here, I may just try winning him over with my skills in the bedroom."

The thought of Devaroe in her bed both excited and annoyed Olivia. Anytime she thought of him inside her, she got all hot and tingly, but she did not want to think about what he might have in mind for her. She thought it would certainly be more pleasurable to him than to her. She still couldn't believe his harsh treatment of her and Magdalena.

Maybe he was just upset over his losses due to the storm, and he was taking it out on the first people who happened to cross his path. Father could be that way if he suffered business setbacks.

Olivia didn't want to dwell on James Devaroe for the moment and smiled at her grinning sister.

"Magda LaMonte," she teased, "you're a shameless little tart."

"What is it they say about when in Rome, do as the Romans do? We live in a quad of brothels. I'm just trying to fit in with our new neighbors." She laughed and slapped Olivia on the back as she unlocked the door to the townhouse.

"You start boiling the chicken, and I'll slice the onions, peppers, and okra for the gumbo," Olivia told her sister and slipped out of her jacket before going to the kitchen and removing things from the icebox. She handed Magdalena the chicken wrapped in brown butcher's paper and took out the crock of butter she would need to sauté the onions, peppers, and shrimp.

The remainder of the afternoon they spent in the kitchen. By the time the clock struck five, a large pot of gumbo simmered on the stove, and biscuits rested on the warming rack above the flat iron top. Olivia also sliced some peaches and whipped some sweetened cream, though that was not the dessert Devaroe had in mind, she was certain.

Magdalena spooned some of the gumbo into the chafing dish from the offensive café. She wrapped some biscuits in a napkin and scooped some of the peaches and cream into a chilled crock. All of this, she carefully stowed in a basket with a handle.

"I think I am going to be on my way, Livvy unless you want me to fix up the table for ya."

"No, you go on ahead, Magda. I can finish this on my own. You're not my maid any longer."

Magdalena picked up the basket, careful not to upset the chaffing dish with the gumbo, and walked toward the door. "If that man starts getting' mean with you, just go to the window and scream. We'll be able to hear ya and come runnin'."

"Thank you, Magda, but I think I can handle Mr. James Devaroe. You go on and have a good time." Olivia watched her sister leave and envied her. Magda and Ben would share the same sweet, tender love she and William had shared. All she had to look for from Devaroe was sated lust on both their parts. There could be no lasting relationship based only upon that.

Olivia set the table with china from the cabinet. It did not compare to the ornate Thibodeaux family set, but it was nice, and the deep-dished plates would be perfect for the rice and gumbo. She added the bread plates, flatware, napkins, and candlesticks. As this was an obligatory dinner with the man who called himself her husband and not a romantic dinner for two people who loved and wanted one another, Olivia omitted any flowers or other ornamentation. Her table was neat but made no illusions to romance.

When the knocker sounded, Olivia had just finished changing from her suit into her dressing gown over her best camisole and bloomers. She hoped all he wanted was dinner and sex. She wished she could be done with him soon.

The knocker sounded for a second time, and she went to the door and opened it. Devaroe, dressed in his more formal black waistcoat and top hat, stood there with roses in his hand. He stepped in, and Olivia shut the door.

"I dressed for dinner," he sneered, taking in her

choice of apparel. "You could have done me the courtesy of doing the same."

"Just having you in my home is courtesy enough in my way of thinking," Olivia retorted. "We made you dinner, and I dressed for your required dessert." She pointed at the table and then her choice of dress.

Devaroe looked around the townhouse, taking in the furnishings and the modest decoration in the place. "And where is your lovely *cousin?* I was hoping she might be joining us for dinner *and* dessert." Devaroe burst out laughing when he saw her blanch at the suggestion. He handed her the roses and walked around her to look into the kitchen.

"Magda went out for the evening." Olivia followed him into the kitchen with the flowers and an empty vase from the mantel. She pumped some water into the vase and arranged the roses before setting them atop the icebox.

Devaroe took them from the icebox and put them into the center of the table between the two candlesticks, which he then lit. He took a seat at the table and undid the buttons of his waistcoat. Olivia brought in a dish of gumbo over rice and placed it on the table. As she stood by the table, Devaroe slipped his hand inside her dressing gown and ran it down over her behind, sending shivers of both pleasure and foreboding through Olivia.

I refuse to enjoy this. If the ass wants to be crude and make this a transaction between a paid woman and her client, then so be it.

"That smells wonderful, wife, and this," he squeezed a butt cheek, "feels wonderful. Perhaps we should have dessert first." He brought his hand around to find the opening between the legs of her bloomers and slid his hand inside to explore the hot wetness there.

He pulled her closer until his cheek rested against her belly, and he pushed two fingers inside her, rotating them in a slow, steady motion that made her moan with both pleasure and uncertainty. Olivia did not want to admit that the man excited and pleasured her, but he did. Olivia wanted to pull away from him and retreat to the safety of the kitchen, but instead, she relaxed and leaned into him as he teased her throbbing cunny. He pulled his finger out of her, massaged the throbbing mound above the slit, and then pushed back into her again with more vigor. With his teeth, he tugged on the ribbon of her camisole until it came free, and he lifted his head from her belly to suck a throbbing nipple into his mouth.

Devaroe practiced at the art of pleasuring a woman, brushed his tongue over her hard nipple with the same motion as he touched her throbbing cunny. Within minutes, Olivia arched into his massaging fingers and pressed herself into his teasing mouth. Sweat dripped off her brow, and she gasped in wicked pleasure with her release. The hot burst of pleasure between her thighs exploded in delicious waves, and she wanted to collapse into his arms.

Devaroe pushed her away and gazed at her with a leering smile. "Now it's my turn, wife." He yanked Olivia down to her knees in front of him, unbuttoned his trousers, and released his erect cock in her face. He pushed her head down until her mouth hovered over the bulbous head. "Kiss it," he demanded as he pushed her mouth down to meet the oozing organ. "Kiss it and lick it clean. Then put it in your sweet little mouth and suck it dry."

Olivia tried to pull back in horror at what he wanted her to do, but he held fast to her head and pushed her head down until her lips met the organ, and she tasted the thick, sticky fluid on her mouth. She pursed her lips and kissed the purple bulb, then hesitantly pushed her tongue out to explore the throbbing head of his thick cock.

"Oh, yes," Devaroe moaned. "Lick it all around the head. Use that tongue, wife."

Olivia did as he instructed, not because she wanted to but because Devaroe gave her no choice, holding her head down on his cock. Then he pushed hard, and it was between her lips and in her mouth completely. He pushed until she gagged on the thick organ but allowed her to pull back a little.

"Open up and take as much as you can," he said breathlessly as he pushed Olivia's head back down onto the stiff organ with his hand twisted in her raven hair. He pushed and pulled. "And don't stop using that tongue. Keep licking my cock," he moaned and pushed and pulled her head up and down on his hot, bulging erection. He pumped his hips, pressed into her mouth, and moaned as she continued to flick her tongue around, teasing the spot just under the head that seemed to elicit the most groans when she played with it. "Oh, yes," he groaned, stiffened his body in the chair, and released his hot, bitter fluid into her mouth.

Olivia gagged as the fluid gushed into her mouth, and she tried to pull back. "Oh, no," Devaroe told her and continued to hold her head tight to his crotch. "I want you to swallow everything I give you. Every damned drop."

With Devaroe's hand gripping her head tight and pushing it into his crotch, Olivia had no choice but to swallow the foul mess that lay on her tongue like runny egg whites. With the realization that he was not going to release her until she did as he told her,

Olivia closed her eyes tight, fought back the urge to gag, and swallowed the warm, bitter fluid.

When he felt her swallow, Devaroe relaxed his grip on Olivia's head, and she sat up. She wiped her mouth on her sleeve and tried to stand. Her neck ached from Devaroe's tight hold on it, and her knees hurt from pressing on the floorboards for so long. He helped her to her feet with a lascivious smile. "You see, wife, I knew that hole was going to pleasure me too. We shall do that before every meal, I think."

Olivia pulled away from him and stumbled into the kitchen, working the pain from her abused knees. She took the biscuits from the warming shelf and picked up the crock of butter. Then Olivia set them both on the counter and went to the sink for some water. She took a sip, washed it around her mouth, and spit it into the sink. It didn't do much to get the taste or feel of him out of her mouth, but it would have to do.

She took the biscuits and butter to the table where Devaroe sat, opening a bottle of wine. He must have chosen one from the rack near the table and found the corkscrew.

"Come now, wife. Let's enjoy this lovely meal together before we retire and enjoy one another for the night." He gave her a lascivious smile and filled their glasses with the dark red wine.

Olivia picked up her glass and drank deeply of the sweet, hearty vintage made from the wild grapes found in the local swamps. It was one of her favorites, and she had purchased several bottles at the market when she'd seen it.

"I don't know how you can abide this backwater swill," Devaroe spat. "We'll have to get some good French vintages if I'm going to be residing here on occasion."

"If you are going to be residing here, you are more than welcome to spend *your* money on whatever you like. I happen to enjoy the Clairvoux wines." She took another drink and set the glass down. The wine helped to refresh her appetite, and she spooned some of the rice and gumbo, thick with chicken and shrimp, onto her plate. Then she buttered a biscuit and laid it on her bread plate.

If I must share my meal with this bastard, I'm going to enjoy it.

Olivia stabbed a shrimp with her fork and stuffed it whole into her mouth. She chewed it and dabbed at the corners of her mouth to wipe at the escaping, spicy juices. The rice, savory with the gumbo sauce, filled her, and she enjoyed every bite.

Devaroe soaked up the sauce with his biscuit and popped it into his mouth, followed by a long drink of the wine.

"Your *cousin* is a fine cook," he sighed and laid his napkin over his empty plate.

"Magdalena didn't cook this," Olivia told him. "I did. She helped with some of the prep, but the recipe is mine, and I made the biscuits. There are peaches and whipped cream if you would care for some."

He looked at the remains of the savory meal and smiled. "Perhaps you will make a passable wife after all. You're a good fuck and a good cook, too? How did a pampered little plantation princess like you learn to do either of those?"

"I had good teachers." She watched him raise an eyebrow and smiled to herself. "Magdalena's mother taught us both to cook. She set us to kitchen chores when we were little and underfoot. As for the other, William was a good teacher. He showed me how to pleasure him while allowing me to experience my pleasure as well."

"You seemed to enjoy your pleasure earlier," he said with a chuckle deep in his throat.

"Yes, but it was the first time you've ever actually allowed my pleasure before pleasuring yourself." Olivia stood and began collecting the dirty plates. "Do you want some peaches?" she asked before carrying the pile of dishes into the kitchen.

"That would be nice, thank you, wife."

Why does he refuse to use my name?

Olivia took the bowl of cold, sliced peaches, and whipped cream from the icebox. Dipping her finger into the cold, fluffy cream and sticking it into her mouth to savor, she was certain the investment in the icebox had been well worth it. Olivia spooned peaches into shallow dessert dishes and topped them with the sweetened whipped cream.

At the table, she found a glass filled with white wine awaiting her. "The red is fine with the gumbo, but peaches and cream deserve a more delicate vintage." Devaroe lifted his glass and smiled over the vase of fragrant roses.

Olivia lifted hers in return and drank. She had to admit that his choice of the sweet, white dessert wine paired much better with the peaches and cream's delicate flavors. They sat quietly, enjoying the dessert, and Olivia looked at Devaroe intently. The man was a conundrum. One minute he was a brutal, foulmouthed thug, and the next, a perfectly refined gentleman of class and taste. She watched him eat the peaches with their sweet cream, savoring his pleasure in the simple treat. She watched him lick the cream from his spoon like a little boy trying to get every last bit of the sweet delight.

He caught her smiling at him and smiled back. "Summer peaches have always been a favorite of mine. My mother's cook whipped cream and sugar together this way to put on top of them." He picked up his glass of wine and drained it. "How much do you anticipate your monthly expenses to be here, Olivia?" he asked, using her name for the first time that day. She liked the way it sounded coming from his lips.

"I can't imagine that food, ice, and household necessities will cost us more than ten dollars. I've already made arrangements with Ben to repaint the house, doors, and shutters. He is going to do that for thirty dollars, including the cost of the paint. He already replaced several roof tiles after the storm." Thinking of Ben reminded her about Blue, and she added, "And keeping my horse and buggy at the livery is four dollars a month."

"Very well, then." He let out a long sigh and pushed back in his chair. "I will have a household account set up for you at the bank and deposit fifty dollars a month into it for your expenses here. That should also cover any unforeseen repairs such as storm-damaged roof tiles."

Olivia was caught off guard for a moment by his generosity.

"Shall we retire to your boudoir now that I may have what is due me as your husband?"

With that, Olivia realized he was not generous at all. He was paying his whore for her services.

❧ 21 ☙

Devaroe followed Olivia up the stairs after she'd cleared the table and straightened the kitchen. He had taken that time to have a smoke in the court-yard. From the window over the sink, she had watched him stare up at the rooms of the neigh-boring townhouses in the quad. Olivia wondered if some of those women were the regulars he'd men-tioned earlier in the day, with just the slightest pang of jealousy. She shook her head at the absurdity of it and finished her chores.

In her room, he opened the French doors and stepped out onto the balcony, bathed in the red glow of the setting sun. "This is a nice house, Olivia. I think I am going to be very happy here. It's a short walk to the harbor and my offices there." He came back in and swept her up into his arms. "And it houses a beautiful woman with a tight cunny, a very tight asshole, and a delicious mouth." He bent and kissed her as he pushed the dressing gown off her shoulders.

Olivia could not deny her attraction to this man and his crude desire to tell her those unseemly things. Once again, when their lips met, she got a lightning

185

jolt that caused a tingling across her lips. She could not remember ever feeling that sensation with William.

Am I just imagining that? I know I felt it the first time, just like he did, but did I just imagine it this time?

Devaroe undid the tiny buttons on her camisole with ease and pushed it off her shoulders to flutter to the floor. She did the same with his silk shirt, though he had to undo the cuffs before she could get the garment off his muscular, tanned body. The last rays of the sun cast a brilliant glow over his rippling muscles of his arms, gleaming with a fine sheen of sweat. The long summer days meant longer hours of heat and humidity.

He pulled the ribbon on her bloomers loose, and they fell to puddle on the floor at her feet. She stepped out of them, and he pushed her down onto the bed. She watched him unbutton his trousers and release his erect penis. Olivia swore she could see the veins pulsing in the hard cock, just like the pulsing of the hard button throbbing between her legs. She slid her feet back, bringing her knees up and letting them fall open so he could see her the way she could see him.

"Wife, you entice like the whores in the other townhouses around you." He fell on her then, burying his face in the curve of her neck, biting and sucking hard. Olivia felt her nipples harden and rise against his hot skin. He felt them too and slid down to suck one into his mouth, nipping it with his teeth until she squealed. James brought a hand up to the other nipple and pinched it between thumb and forefinger. The attention to both nipples brought a gushing sensation of pleasure between her thighs, and she longed for him to be in her, but he denied her momentarily while he continued to pinch and suck her nipples.

He traced a finger down her taut belly through the hair above her womanhood and into her. "You are so wet, wife. Just wet enough, I'd bet." He sighed and slid into her so slow she could feel every inch of him stretching her as he wet his erection with her juices. "Oh, yes," he breathed in her ear, and she felt him pull out of her cunny and drop down to her other hole. He shoved into her and moaned with pleasure. "Wife, you have the tightest asshole in all of New Orleans." He pumped into her, and she winced in pain. The wince excited him, and he pushed farther into her, pumping faster and faster with his ballocks bouncing off her ass cheeks.

Olivia looked up at his face. With his dusky blue eyes closed, he smiled and breathed heavily through his aquiline nose. James grabbed her delicate, slim hips and pulled her closer to him as the power of his thrusting pushed her up in the bed and away from him. He opened his eyes and saw her studying his face.

"Shall I finish this in your tight cunny or your pretty pink mouth?" he asked without slowing. "Your cunny." He smiled. "It's too late to get it to your mouth." Without missing a stroke, Devaroe pulled out of her ass and shoved into her throbbing cunny.

Olivia massaged herself in readiness for his release and wrapped her legs around his waist. She pulled herself into his every thrust, luxuriating in the long, hard cock pummeling her to that peak of exquisite pleasure, which, when it came, brought a guttural explosion from her throat as the waves of pleasure pulsed through her groin and her heart pounded.

Her groan of pleasure brought on his release,

and he wailed like a wild man, falling on her to nuzzle her ear. "Was that better for you?" he whispered and nibbled at the lobe of her ear. "I let you go first."

"Yes, thank you," Olivia sighed and wrapped her arms around his shoulders, her hands resting on his spine and scratching it in gentle circles with her nails.

"Um, that feels good," he moaned, "don't stop."

She didn't. They lay there together like that for a long time. Olivia watched the sky fade from red to pink, then a deep lavender until finally, stars twinkled in blackness.

"James." She breathed his name and again when he did not respond. "James, I need to use the privy." She pushed at him, and he rolled off her. She pulled herself up, threw her legs over the side of the bed, and stood. She felt his fluid running out of her and slicking the insides of her quivering thighs.

Olivia hurried to the privy closet in the dark and tripped on a pile of clothing. She recognized her dressing gown's feel and bent and picked it up to carry with her to the privy closet. Olivia dipped a washcloth in the water in the washbasin as she sat on the commode chair, first washing the sweat from her face and neck, then attending to the mess between her legs. Her eyes adjusted to the darkness, and when she brought the cloth away from her backside, she didn't see any dark splotches there. No blood this time. She threw the soiled cloth back into the bowl.

Olivia thought about lighting the lamp in the privy closet but did not want to attract mosquitos through the open doors. The damp night air felt nice, and she didn't want to close the doors if she didn't have to. If they didn't light a lamp, maybe the little bloodsuckers would stay outside. The other downside of having the doors open was the occasional whiff of refuse from the muck pits in the alley and the street. She tried to keep their hole coated with lime to manage the smell, but others in the neighborhood did not, and the stench of human waste ruined many a lovely evening on the balconies of Basin Street. The storm's heavy rains had flushed and cleaned the city's streets and alleys, sending the filth to drain into the Gulf and the nearby river.

Crawling back into her bed, Olivia pulled a light coverlet up over her body more to shield it from mosquitoes than for the need of warmth and snuggled in next to a softly snoring James Devaroe. Her feelings for this man perplexed her. Her body yearned for his attentions, but she also experienced revulsion at his crudeness and his delight in rough treatment. He was just so much like her father—perhaps too much.

Olivia refused to allow this man to treat her how her father had treated her mother for all their years together. Had her mother ever enjoyed the attentions of her father in the bedroom? Had they ever been in love? Marie had told her that she'd loved her husband, but Olivia could not fathom how that could have been true. Her parents' marriage, an arrangement between families, had never been a loving one, as far as Olivia could remember. Armand Thibodeaux regularly bedded with slaves and white-trash women of the bayou without regard to her mother's feelings. He kept whores in the city and possibly a mistress or two there also. Then there were his drunken rages and the beatings that followed. Olivia had sworn all her life that she would never be treated that way by a man.

But look at me now. I'm allowing myself to be treated like a common whore by a man with the same brutal proclivities as my father. What kind of fool am I?

She had been so very lucky to find her sweet

William. He had been the sort of husband every young girl dreamed of having. He had been educated with gentle manners and put Olivia first in all things. The only real argument they ever had was when he had enlisted. Her fear of losing him had caused her to take on some of her father's mannerisms, and she'd stormed at William for being willing to leave her alone. At his wake, she'd stormed at him again, pounding on his casket with her fists and cursing the war, the Yankees, Jefferson Davis, and William. Georgia had had to dose her with a sleeping potion to calm her, and she had missed the actual burial mass.

Now she lay here in their bed with another man. Devaroe was the only other man to share her bed or her body besides William. He rolled and draped an arm over Olivia's body, pulling her close.

"Come here to me, wife," he whispered before drifting back into sleep.

Olivia snuggled into his body. He smelled of Bay Rum cologne and stale tobacco smoke. He smelled like a man, and Olivia had to admit that she'd missed having a man in her bed. His soft, even breathing lulled her to sleep.

His sucking on her breast woke her. The shadows cast by the building told her the sun had risen, but only just. "Good morning, wife," he whispered, noticing she had opened her eyes. He slid a hand down between her legs and went back to sucking and biting her nipple. His finger found that sensitive knot between her thighs and massaged it, causing her to moan and arch into his touch. Olivia felt his hardness against her thigh and reached over to caress it. He bit down on her nipple, causing her to yelp in pain.

Her reaction excited him, and he sucked and

chewed harder. His hand between her thighs explored, and after inserting two fingers without a response, he tried three. She yelped, and he withdrew his hand. "Tell me you want my cock in you," he said as he positioned himself over her body. "Say it," he demanded and pinched her nipple hard.

"I want your cock in me," she said with some reservation.

"Say it as though you actually mean it, wife. I want you to beg me for it, Olivia. Beg me to put it in all your pretty little holes."

Olivia conceded to his unusual foreplay and found herself in the throes of ecstasy twice. It amazed her, but the combination of the crude talk and his demanding actually excited *her*. Devaroe got up to visit the privy closet, and Olivia rolled on her side, opened the drawer of the bedside table, and rummaged through it. When he returned, she held out her hand to him.

"I have a gift for you." She offered her clenched hand.

"What, another?" He smiled and cupped his hands beneath hers. When Olivia dropped what she concealed, his eyes went wide. "I thought I had irretrievably lost at the bottom of that pond," he gasped, staring at the pearl ring. "How…?" He clenched the lovely pearl ring in his fist and held it to his chest with his eyes closed. Olivia watched his lips moving in a silent prayer of thanks. "I never thought to see this precious family token again in my lifetime. How did you retrieve it?"

Olivia smiled at his joy. "Jimbo, our groom at Sweet Rewards, spent nearly a whole Sunday diving to the bottom of the pond and running his hands through the muck until he found it, along with some silver coins and a fork." She laughed.

"I owe this Jimbo my undying gratitude." He opened his fist and stared at the ring resting on his palm. "And you, of course, wife." He took her hand and positioned the pearl ring to place on her finger when he noted William's ring already there. "I will not remove that," Devaroe told her, crestfallen. "It must mean more to you than this one ever could."

Twisting the tiny gold band on her finger, a wave of pain and grief overcame Olivia, and the sting of tears flooded her eyes.

He's right, of course. William's ring will always mean more. But then, why do I feel so upset that I've disappointed him? James Devaroe will never be able to take William's place in my heart—maybe in my bed, but never in my heart.

Devaroe collected his discarded clothing and dressed in haste. "I will trouble you no more today, Mrs. Montgomery. I will open the household account on Monday. You can retrieve the passbook from Henri at the bank any time after that." He stormed down the stairs, and Olivia heard the door slam as he left the townhouse. Voices on the street below her window and the door's reopening alerted her of Magdalena's return.

"Did that man hurt you again, Livvy?" her sister bellowed up to her. "If he did, the bastard be gettin' some of that special gumbo next time he visits."

Olivia wiped her eyes, wrapped herself in her dressing gown, and went down the stairs in her bare feet. "I am fine, Magda."

"Why are you cryin' then?" Magdalena grabbed Olivia by the chin, turning her head from left to right. "Did he slap you around again?"

"No, he didn't hit me." Olivia went into the kitchen to put water into the pot to boil some coffee. "I gave him his ring back."

"That should have made the bastard happy." She

began taking dishes from her basket and returning them to the cabinets.

"It did. It made Mr. Devaroe very happy," Olivia sighed.

"So why are you cryin' like a baby?" she asked and stood her ground until Olivia answered her.

"He wanted to put it back on my finger, but..." Olivia held up her hand with William's ring.

"Oh." Magdalena picked up the basket and carried it to the storage area's door beneath the stairs, where they kept it. "And did he want to put *his* wedding ring back on?"

Olivia wiped her eyes again and put a smile on her face. "He couldn't have if he'd wanted to. It's still in the drawer of my night table back at Sweet Rewards. How was your evening?"

Magdalena threw her head back, and a broad smile creased her face. "Olivia, our little Ben ain't so little no more."

"I know. He's as big as a house." Olivia saw the mischievous twinkle in her sister's eyes and giggled. "Oh," she said in understanding, "oh, my."

❦ 22 ❦

A few mornings after Devaroe's visit, Olivia woke to the aroma of frying bacon. The rich, hearty scent usually made Olivia's mouth water with anticipation. Still, that morning it sent her flying into the privy closet to bend over the commode chair and empty her stomach. She knelt over the seat for some time, trying to remember what they'd eaten the night before to bring on such violent heaving.

She finally stood, wiped her mouth and face with a cool cloth, and trudged down the stairs. "I think that gumbo went bad," she said and went to the sink for some water. Magdalena stared at Olivia's blanched face and smiled.

"When was your cycle due, Miss Livvy? That gumbo's been in that icebox since you cooked it, and I smelled it good before heatin' it up last night. I think that mornin' pukes is from something other than bad gumbo. You haven't washed a dirty clout since we left Sweet Rewards."

Thinking back on it, Olivia realized Magda was correct. Her last monthly cycle had been before the party at Sweet Rewards when she'd first met James Devaroe. That was over two months ago. She suddenly felt light-headed and dropped into one of the chairs at the round dining table. "Oh, my God."

"Daddy's going to be mighty happy with you, Liv. If you got a boy in that belly, he'd be shootin' off fireworks over the damned Bayou Tesche."

"Must I remind you, sister, that I don't have a husband any longer? Mother had the marriage annulled."

"So, when that riverboat man of yours comes back to town, drag him down to St. Louis and get married again. Ain't no big deal." Magdalena shrugged her shoulders and forked bacon out of the skillet. "How many eggs you want?"

The thought of runny eggs turned her stomach again, and she ran for the alley door to heave into the offal pit. The odor rising from there only brought on more, and she stood in the alley, braced on the wall, vomiting for almost twenty minutes before returning to the table and resting her head on her arms with a long moan. Magdalena brought her a wet cloth, and she wiped her mouth and face.

"No, weren't no bad gumbo." Magdalena laughed at her sister's obvious discomfort.

"Oh, hush, Magda. When was your last monthly? I haven't seen you washing any clouts, either."

"I started mine last night," she said with a relieved sigh. "No little Jimbos or cane-field niggers in me."

"Well, you better take precautions, or there will be little Bens."

"And what would be so terribly wrong with that?" Magdalena cracked eggs into the hot skillet.

"His mother knows your origins. Do you think she would stand for it?"

"That woman is at death's door," Magdalena

said as she walked back into the kitchen to rinse out the cloth. "But Miss Evangeline always liked me. She never treated me any differently than she treated you."

"We were children then, not adults. Do you think she'd be pleased about the possibility of a Negro grandchild? You have a goodly amount of white blood, but any child of yours could still be born dark."

"I know, and I wouldn't do that to Ben," Magdalena sighed, and a tear ran down her cheek. "I almost think I was happier bein' a house nigger sometimes."

"Magda," Olivia took her sister's hand and held it to her lips, "there are plenty of men that have mixed blood in this city. You can find one, and it won't make any difference if a child is born dark-skinned with nappy hair."

Someone tapped on the glass of the front door, and they looked up to see Ben's smiling face at the window. Magdalena jumped up, wiped her eyes, and fled back into the kitchen. Olivia opened the door, and Ben came bounding through in his overalls, and a faded blue cotton shirt with the sleeves rolled up over his bulging biceps.

"Smells good in here. Is breakfast ready?"

"We have bacon, hard-fried eggs, biscuits, and coffee," Magdalena called from the kitchen. "Livvy, can you get the butter, cream, and jam out of the icebox while I dish this all up?"

Olivia went to the icebox and took out the cold items, hoping her stomach would not decide to burst forth again when she smelled the contents of the icebox. The spicy aroma of the leftover gumbo wafted up to her nose, along with that of the raw catfish, but thankfully, her stomach remained calm.

"Liv, I was wondering if you'd decided on the colors you want for the paint. I'd like to go down and get it mixed. We should have a few nice clear days, and I thought I'd get started." Ben took a seat at the table, and Magdalena brought in cups and the steaming coffee pot. She sat the hot pot on a pad and whipped around back into the kitchen without looking Ben in the face. Olivia watched his eyes, full of hurt, follow her as she sped away.

"I think I want to stay with the butter-yellow for the body of the house," Olivia told him as she poured their coffee, "but I want to change the doors and shutters from green to blue that matches the slate tiles on the roof."

"That's a good idea. It will give the place a fresh look. I've been scraping the shutters, and they were blue at one time. I peeled off a few layers and saw some blue." He leaned into Olivia. "Is Magda alright? Did I do something to upset her?" he whispered with a worried look on his broad face.

Olivia shook her head and turned to smile at her sister, who carried in plates filled with food for the three of them. "I think we'll keep the balcony rails black. What do you think, Magda?"

"They wouldn't look right anything but black. Maybe if we were painting the house blue, I'd say white for the railings, but with yellow, they have to be black."

"I agree," Ben said, digging into his eggs after buttering his biscuits and smearing them with jam.

Someone knocked on the French doors. One of them pushed open, and Nell popped in her pretty blonde head. "Good morning. I thought I saw Ben coming up the walk." She smiled at the big man, which earned her a withering glance from Magdalena. "He told me y'all were going to be repainting your place. I think I want to have mine done, too. What colors are you doing this one?" Olivia told her their choices, and Nell smiled. That sounds lovely, but I think I want to go with a pastel orange like the color of a conch shell with white shutters and iron-work. The slates on my roof are such a light gray, they look white, and I have all those pots of orange lilies."

"Doesn't your landlord have something to say about all that?" Magdalena asked the thin young woman dressed in her usual pink attire.

"That old skin-flint doesn't care what we do as long as we pay for it." Nell stepped completely into the room and shut the door. "Did I see James De-varoe here the other evening?" she asked Olivia.

"Yes, he's a friend of my father's. Do you know him well?" Olivia stabbed a bit of egg with enough force to scoot her plate on the table. She glanced up at Magdalena, who had a smirk on her face as she chewed.

"He's a business acquaintance," Nell told her with a nervous grin. "Ben, if you'll drop by later, we can work out the particulars. You might want to stop over at Sally's, too. I think she wants some painting done inside." Nell opened the door and slipped out as quickly as she'd come.

"Do the girls pay well for your services, Ben?" Magdalena teased him bitterly.

"Magda, I've been doin' little chores around here for some time now. As Nell said, that bastard who bought up the places don't want to spend a penny on them. If the girls want the places kept up, they have to pay for it, and then he wants their rent and a little extra, as well. If you know what I mean?" He blushed, and Olivia had to choke back a giggle.

"Oh, I know exactly what you mean, Ben

Benoit," Magdalena snapped and dropped the coffee pot onto the table.

"The girls pay what I ask," he said, still blushing, "and I never ask for anything extra."

"That's good, Ben." Olivia smiled at him. "We understand."

"It's just that since Papa died, we need the extra money to pay for Mama's medicines. I give my aunt a little every month for her upkeep too."

"I'm sorry. Is your mama much worse?" Olivia asked, thinking about her own sick mother.

"My aunt says the doctors are not hopeful of a recovery. At least she's finally seeing a doctor now, though." He sighed as he filled his cup with coffee. "She suffered another apoplexy and cannot leave her bed. She's ready to join Papa, I think," he said sadly and drained his coffee cup. He stood, walked to Magdalena, and kissed her cheek before going out the French doors into the sunny courtyard where Nell stood with some of the other women.

"Damn that little blonde bitch and her pots of orange flowers," Magdalena growled and pulled her napkin from her lap to throw it onto her empty plate. "And don't you go laughin' at me, Olivia Thibodeaux. I saw the color drain from your lily-white cheeks when Miss Nell said Devaroe was a *business acquaintance*. Your ears were blowin' out steam like that coffee pot just off the stove."

Olivia stuck her tongue out at her sister and collected plates from the table. "We should walk down to the bank on Lafayette and see if Devaroe opened an account for us. I don't know about you, but I could use some fresh air."

"What fresh air?" Magdalena huffed.

They washed, dried, and put away the dishes before changing into respectable suits to wear, strolling out into the city. The thick, stagnant air in New Orleans sent most people who could afford it out to Grande Isle or into the cooler, less crowded bayous where the fears of cholera and yellow fever did not haunt them.

The miasma of stinking filth in the streets and the byproducts of hundreds crowded together in close quarters did not make for pleasant summer living in the city. Olivia longed for the cooler months to come when the sun would shine and soft breezes would blow in off the Gulf without the fears of thunderous storms. On those days, she could leave her doors open without being plagued by flies and mosquitoes or sit in the courtyard and read. Those lazy days of fall and early winter were her favorites.

At the old bank building on Lafayette Street, the elderly banker told Olivia her husband, James Devaroe, had opened a household account for her to draw funds. Olivia withdrew thirty dollars to pay Ben for the painting and another fifty from her other account to have in her bag.

"I will change the name on this account from Montgomery," he told her with a smile, "to Devaroe. I did not realize you and Mr. Devaroe had wed until he informed me of it. Congratulations, James Devaroe, is a good customer of the bank. It is a shame about his losses in the storm. Though I'm happy to say, his surety company has already paid off his ships' outstanding loans, however. We are happy to be able to write new ones for the rebuilding of his fleet."

Olivia smiled at the old man for his compliments and left the building.

"Well," Magdalena said with a giggle, "Mrs. Devaroe, how long before you start receiving visitors? I am sure all the fine ladies of New Orleans will want to come by and offer their heartfelt congratulations on your nuptials with the fine Mr. James Devaroe."

"Oh, hush, Magda." Olivia grimaced as her belly began to roil once more. She took a deep breath and continued toward the townhouse, where Ben busied himself with scraping paint from the window sills, doors, and shutters to prepare for the new paint. "When we get home, I am going to make some lemonade. We still have some lemons, don't we?"

"There's a whole bag full in the pantry. Lemonade sounds good. I'll be glad when this summer is over and done. It's been a frightful hot one so far." Magdalena waved up at Ben with a coy smile before going into the house.

Olivia went upstairs, opened the doors, and stepped out onto the balcony where Ben sweated over his labors. She opened her bag, took out thirty dollars, and handed the bills to the big blond man. "Here's the money for the painting, Ben."

"Thank you, Olivia. Most won't pay until I've finished the job." He pocketed the money and went back to his scraping. "Is everything alright with Magda? She was real quiet this morning."

"It's nothing you did, Ben. It's just some female concerns." Olivia smiled and went back into her room.

"Is she with child?" Ben asked, startling her.

"No, she's not pregnant. We were just discussing what she might do if that should happen."

"I'd marry her, Olivia. I love Magda. I always have." Ben wiped the sweat from his forehead with a paint-stained kerchief.

"I know that Ben and she feels the same," Olivia assured him, "but there are other things to think about there. Even though you are very fair-skinned, any child she might conceive with you could be born dark like her mother and grandmother. Just because you are both fair-complected does not guarantee a fair-skinned child. She does not want to cause you any embarrassment. There is also the worry that if people found Magdalena to be colored and passing herself off as white, she could be whipped or worse. *Charivari* can be very nasty and even deadly. She might just get a public whipping, but a mob of angry people might even lynch her for it."

"I've been thinkin' on that, and I think we just might move out to St. Martinsville. I hear folks out there don't hold with that nonsense. We could live there as man and wife without worry."

"We were thinking of your mother, Ben. What would she say about you marrying a Negress?" Olivia watched his face cloud, thinking of his ailing mother.

"Mama has always known how I feel about Magda. We have discussed it, and she told me to follow my heart. Life is too short to live by other people's rules about who can love who. She has always loved Magda the same as she loves you."

"Are you going to ask Magda to marry then?" Joy for her sister flooded her heart. Olivia studied Ben, and pride swelled in her breast for the brave young man who was willing to buck the system for the woman he loved and move away to a place he didn't know so he could be with her. She could see why William wanted to look after him during the war.

"Her birthday is next month. I'm going to ask her then." Ben smiled and went back to the balcony and his work.

❧ 23 ❧

Bouts of morning sickness continued to plague Olivia for the next few weeks, and she worried that she was losing weight because of it.

"Look at this," she complained to Magdalena one morning when the dress she chose hung on her loosely, "I look like a scarecrow in a bean patch."

"I wouldn't worry none about that. In a few months, you're going to look like you *ate* the bean patch." Magdalena laughed as she poured Olivia some tea to have with her dry biscuit, the only thing she could generally tolerate in the mornings.

Though Olivia had not had a monthly, she had begun to wonder if this was pregnancy or some summer malady like malaria or yellow fever.

"You got no fever, Livvy," Magdalena grimaced when Olivia brought up these alternatives. "What you got is a baby in your belly. It's been almost three months. It'll be passin' pretty soon. When is that riverboat man husband of yours 's'pose to be back in town?"

"It's been over a month," Olivia sighed. "I suspect he'll be back down here any time." For the past two weeks, Olivia had run through her mind, over

and over again, how she was going to tell James Devaroe she carried his child. A letter from her mother
had arrived the week after the morning heaves' on-
set, confirming their marriage annulment.

*What if he no longer wants to have me as his wife? What
if the lure of Sweet Rewards is no longer enough to tempt him?
What if my continuing to wear William's ring was too much
of an insult to him?* All these things plagued Olivia at
night in her bed, chasing sleep away.

The weak scrawl of her mother's once beautiful
flowery handwriting also worried her. In her letter,
Marie Thibodeaux assured her daughter that she
was well and overseeing the household as usual,
though Olivia seriously doubted it.

"Magda, I'm going to go up and take a nap. I
didn't sleep well last night with the heat."

"*Mais oui, Cherie,*" Magdalena said and cleared
away the teacup and saucer from the table, "go and
rest. I am heating water for the wash. Just toss your
dirty things down the stairs."

Olivia trudged up the stairs, each foot heavier
with every step. Fatigued in the stifling heat that
hung like a damp blanket over them, she scooped up
her dirty laundry from its basket and pitched it down
the stairs. Olivia stood for a few moments in front of
the open doors hoping to catch even a little breeze,
but there was none. She crumpled onto the bed,
using her toes to pull her slippers off by the heels.
Pulling her knees up into a fetal position, Olivia
drifted off into fitful sleep.

In the maze of chaotic dreams, Devaroe argued
with her. He accused her of lying about her child's
paternity, claiming it must be the child of Simon
Montrose and not his at all. He yelled at her, and
then he spoke softly, lovingly even. Then, the sting of
his slaps on her face made her cry out in pain and

humiliation. She saw his beautiful ring on her finger again, and then in her dream, he pulled it from her finger, yelling at her and slapping her again. Tears ran from her eyes.

Olivia woke with someone shaking her by the shoulders. She opened her eyes to see James Devaroe bending over her. He pulled her close and held her to him. "Olivia, my darling, Magdalena told me the wonderful news. We are going to have a child?" He wrapped his big arms around her and hugged her tight.

"Did she tell you everything?" Olivia asked, pushing back from him to look into his eyes. "Did she tell you the priest annulled the marriage?"

"Yes, yes, but that's of no consequence. We can go to see the priest at St. Louis Neuf Cathedral this very afternoon. You are my wife, Olivia." He lifted her hand. In place of William's gold band, she now beheld the pearl ring with its two little yellow diamonds. He must have exchanged them while she slept and dreamed.

"Come now." He pulled her up from the bed. "Dress in something pretty, and we shall go see the priest and make this completely official." He looked over his shoulder to Magdalena. "You as well, *cousin*. You know she will want to have her family there as a witness."

The lavender silk Josephine dress remained at Sweet Rewards, so Olivia opted for a red satin gown she'd worn for last Christmas's festivities. The sleeves were long, but the red with her raven hair shone exquisitely. The bodice shimmered with glass beads of red and gold, the high collar and cuffs were trimmed with red French lace dusted with gold along its scalloped edges.

Magdalena emerged in her green suit that set off

the green of her eyes, and Olivia handed her the jade ring. "Ben is coming too," she told them as she slipped the ring onto her right hand. "He just ran down to his apartment to change." The broad-shouldered blond had been working on the shutters outside Magdalena's room when the impromptu wedding was announced and invited himself to come along with Magdalena.

Olivia bent in to whisper to Devaroe, who frowned at the delay. "I think he's going to propose."

Devaroe screwed up his face in dismay. "You can't be serious. Does he know she's a Negress?"

"Of course he knows," Olivia said, grimacing, and led him out into the courtyard where they could speak more freely. "We all grew up together here. He's been in love with Magda since we were children."

"I don't know that I can condone this," he said with a shake of his dark head. "It's against the law and, I believe, against God."

"And the great James Devaroe has never done anything against the law," Olivia demanded and gestured toward the other townhouses that housed the prostitutes, "or against God? Anyhow, Governor Kellogg has changed all those old laws against interracial marriage here in Louisiana."

"But we could be disgraced if it ever became known that we participated in this fraud."

"For God's sake, James, you pirated vessels on the high seas and probably committed murder. You own a business. Tell me you've never committed fraud. How many of those old tubs sunk there in the harbor were insured for more than they were worth?" Olivia stormed with a scowl on her pale face.

"Very well, wife." He cleared his throat and attempted to sound gruff. "You are a shrewd negotiator. I will keep this confidence for you." He kissed her forehead and patted her belly. "I do not want to see you lynched by a mob of Democrats with our son in there." They walked back inside hand-in-hand.

Olivia smiled as they sat on the settee together, awaiting Ben's arrival. Abruptly Devaroe stood and moved toward the stairs. "I need to use your privy closet," he said and bounded up the stairs, passing Magdalena on her way down.

"Where is he goin' in such an all-fired hurry?" she asked, straightening her jacket he'd pulled on his way past her on the narrow stairs.

"Privy," Olivia answered. "I think he might be nervous."

Magdalena answered the door when Ben tapped, and she squealed when he pulled her out to join him on the sidewalk. Devaroe came back down the stairs and was about to push the door closed when they heard a loud, shrill scream from outside.

"Yes, yes, yes," they heard Magdalena shrieking.

"I guess he did it," Devaroe said, but he was not smiling.

"James, if you're not comfortable with this, we can do it another time, or not at all." Olivia sighed. "I don't think I want to be married to a man who has such leanings toward the White League."

"I am not White League," he protested, "but I am a Democrat, and the whole idea of a good white man marrying a Negress rubs me the wrong way."

"Look at her, James; she's whiter than you are."

"It's not the shade of her skin, wife. It's her blood. You cannot deny her blood is Negro, and any child they may have will be Negro because of the blood, and I can't countenance it."

Olivia looked at him in shock. Without hesitating, she pulled his ring from her finger and handed it to him on her way back up to her room. "Get out of my house, James Devaroe, and don't you ever come back."

She heard him following but continued up. "Here," he said coldly. Olivia turned, and he held out William's band to her. "I was going to give this to Ben to use. I didn't think you'd mind." He dropped the ring on the stair at her feet, turned, and left. She heard the door slam and came close to following after him but did not. She bent, picked up the ring, and held it in her hand tightly as hot tears coursed down her cheeks.

Magdalena and Ben came into the townhouse together, grinning. "Where is *your* man going, Olivia?" Magdalena asked. "I thought we were going to the church."

Olivia wiped tears from her face with her red sleeve and came back down the stairs. "There will be no wedding between that man and me today or any other."

"What the hell happened now? He was pleased as could be when I told him about the baby. What did you do to change his mind?" Magdalena demanded.

"He didn't think it was his. Did he?" Olivia asked, remembering snippets of harsh words from her dreams.

"Did he say that to you? I told him he was ridiculous even thinking such a fool thing."

"It's of no consequence now, Magda," Olivia told her sister and went to Ben. "I'm happy for the two of you, though. You should go to the church." She reached up with the pretense of an innocent kiss of congratulations on his cheek but whispered in his ear and slipped the gold band into his hand.

"Off with you now, go to the church and make

this official." Olivia hugged her sister tightly. This would mean losing Magdalena for good. Since childhood, they had been together, only separated while Olivia attended finishing school in New Orleans in her early teens before meeting William and marrying late in her fifteenth year. Then Magdalena had come to live with them here. Now she would marry and move in with Ben. Her sister, her companion, her friend would be gone from her side.

Feeling light-headed at the thought, Olivia sat. She leaned back on the settee and waved goodbye to Magdalena and Ben as they went out the door, both wearing broad smiles. In her heart, she wished them well but found herself overwhelmed with grief and loss. Suddenly a fluttering in her midsection caught her by surprise.

Is it gas or something I ate? The fluttering came again, and she put a hand over her lower abdomen, realizing with a start that it must be the babe rolling around in there. *He's telling me to think about him. He's here. He won't be leaving me, not for a good long time.* Tears filled her eyes. *I have more than just myself to think of now.* Olivia clutched at her abdomen, and the light fluttering occurred again.

"Very well, child," Olivia cooed. "I will begin thinking of your needs over my own." She stood again and went to the kitchen, where she poured a glass of milk from the icebox. Olivia drank it down, rinsed the glass, and went up to her room, where she changed out of the red dress and into a comfortable, cooler day dress.

Out on the sidewalk, she looked up at the townhouse's façade, scraped by Ben of loose and flaking paint. In her mind's eye, Olivia saw it with the warm butter-yellow paint and slate-blue shutters and doors soon to come.

But will this be a good place to raise a child? Olivia could hear the raucous laughter of drunken men from the tavern down the block and a carriage splashed stinking filth onto her skirt as it passed. The laughter of whores drifted down from the balcony of the townhouse next door. *No, this is no place to raise a child. Should I return to Sweet Rewards then? It is a place where a child can run and play without the filth of sewers, drunks, and whores at least.*

Olivia felt the flutter in her belly once again and reached for it protectively. *Very well, child, we will return to Sweet Rewards. Perhaps your Grandmama will want to live long enough to hold you in her arms.* She shook the muck from her skirt and returned inside.

$\maltese$ 24 $\maltese$

"What do you mean you're going home?" Magdalena demanded as she stood watching Olivia pack her cases. "I thought you wanted to get away from that damned place for good."

"I did, Magda," Olivia said and raised her hand to her abdomen, "but I have another to consider now." She rested a hand over her belly protectively. "Can I raise a child in a house surrounded by nothing but filth, drunks, and whores? At Sweet Rewards, he will have room to run and play, at least. And possibly, with a grandchild to look forward to, Mother will hang onto life a little longer. I want to be able to put a grandchild into her arms before she passes from this world." Olivia's voice choked with a sob, and she allowed the tears that had been welling in her eyes to fall. "Daddy will be pleased."

"And if it's not a boy," Magdalena said with a frown, "what will he go and do if that child in your belly comes out a girl?"

Olivia had considered that. If the child were a boy, she knew her father would embrace it with joy, but she did not know what his reaction would be if it were a girl. He might send them both back to New

Orleans, his disgraced daughter, and her bastard child. With no husband to explain the existence of the child, Olivia would be a burden. He would not be able to procure her a husband of genteel birth. Olivia imagined he would name one of her cousins his heir and be done with her and her bastard girl-child. A boy, he would legitimize with his condoning their betrothal pre-marriage sex, but Olivia did not think he would do the same for a girl.

It was a chance she would have to take. If she bore a girl and her father denied her, she would have no choice but to return to the townhouse. Perhaps she could sell the place to the other houses' owner and find something in a better part of town. If it were not for the hope of allowing her mother the joy of a grandchild, Olivia would do just that now and stay in the city.

"I have a plan if that happens," Olivia said and told her sister about the idea of selling the townhouse and relocating to a better part of the city. "I still want you and Ben to move in here, though. It's going to be months before we have to face that." Olivia folded the last of her things into the case and closed it. "You're gonna have to sit on this one, too," she laughed, "so I can buckle it."

"This is most certainly better than Ben's room over the livery," Magdalena said as she moved to sit on the bulging case. "If me and Ben have a babe, we couldn't stay up there. It hardly has enough room for the two of us as it is. I can have Ben make some in-quiries about selling to that Matisse fella. Ben knows him and can negotiate a good price when the time comes. We are talkin' on movin' out to St. Mar-tinsville anyhow."

"That's a good idea, but don't get ahead of things. If I have a boy, I'll be staying at Sweet Rewards. If it's a girl, I'll get word to you, and then he can begin negotiations for the sale. I'll be in childbed for a while after the birth before I can travel anyhow."

"What about that riverboat man of yours?" Magdalena asked as they carried bags down the stairs to where Ben waited to pack them into her buggy. "What do you want me to say if he comes round askin' after you and the babe?"

"I seriously doubt James Devaroe will be coming back around looking for me." Olivia had gone to her bank and found that Devaroe had closed the household account he'd opened for her. "He does not care about anything for his child or me. You can tell him whatever you like. He won't have the gall to show his face at Sweet Rewards after running out on me the way he did. Daddy, if he gets his heir, would pepper his ass with lead. The other we'll deal with when we must."

"Be careful, Liv." Magdalena hugged her in the predawn glow. "People in this city are goin' damned crazy now. Ben said he heard the White League is gatherin' troops out on Iberville Road to march in and throw Governor Kellogg out of the office and put that Democrat nigger-hater into the State House in his place. You take the long way round to get out of town to avoid that lot."

"I'm not worried, Magda. Kellogg has his Black Militia to guard him and the city. President Grant isn't going to let the Democrats and their White League take Louisiana."

The dawn was just breaking in the East as Olivia set Blue on the road north out of New Orleans and toward Sweet Rewards. She had no idea what her reception would be when she got there, but Olivia knew she needed to do this for the child growing inside her. Getting out of the city now would be a good thing with the political tensions mounting between the Republican Governor Kellogg and the Democrats who wanted to put their own man in office who would stop the freedoms being allowed Negroes by Kellogg's administration. The Democrats blamed the last Republican governor for giving the Negroes the vote and signing them up as Republicans to get Kellogg into office in the first place. They claimed their man was the rightful governor because they didn't recognize the Negro votes.

She passed through a few roadblocks on her way out of the city, but things went smoothly once she was well north of town. The last of the summer heat made an appearance, and Olivia began to sweat under the jacket of her traveling suit by early afternoon. The days had begun to shorten, but she was determined to make it to Sweet Rewards that night. Ben had mounted a lamp on the buggy so she could light it and travel after sunset if she must. Olivia remembered the theft of their goods at the King's Inn on their way to New Orleans and did not intend to have a reoccurrence by stopping there.

She came very close to pulling into the horrible place for a bite of food when she and Blue came to it, but she thought better of it as she saw the sun was beginning to dip lower on the horizon. Instead, she snapped the reins and set Blue at a faster pace. Olivia had only been away for a short of three months but had almost forgotten how wonderful the air smelled outside the city. She breathed deeply and enjoyed the sight of the leaves beginning to change colors on the oaks, maples, and sweetgums. Deer crossed her path a few times, and the chirping of birds in the hedges reminded her that she was back in the swamps.

A few miles past the inn, a group of men stopped

her progress with barrels blocking the road. Olivia pulled Blue to a halt and waited for a man in a tattered waistcoat and straw hat, who barked orders as if he were the leader of this motley assortment, to walk up to the buggy.

"What you doin' out here on the road so late, Miss?" he asked and eyed the cases stacked in the back with interest.

"I am on my way home to Sweet Rewards," she told him bluntly.

He eyed her closely then and took hold of Blue's bridle. "You that daughter of Armand Thibodeaux's who killed Simon Montrose and his daddy?" he asked as he walked closer to the buggy, running a hand along Blue's sweaty flank.

"I did not kill Simon's father," Olivia answered, irritated by the man's impertinence. "Mr. Montrose died of an unfortunate heart attack at my wedding."

"But you admit to killing Simon?" he asked with a sneer. "You killed him because you're a nigger-lover is what we heared." He tilted his head toward the others manning the barricades. Then he had his hands on her, pulling her down from the buggy onto the red gravel of the road.

"Get your hands off me, sir," Olivia demanded and jerked loose from his grasp while the others looked on, twittering with laughter. She could smell liquor on the man's breath and suspected the whole group had spent the day passing around a jug or two.

"You gonna let that bitch by, Mason?" one of the others said, laughing. "Why don't we make her pay a toll to pass?" Olivia heard them hooting their ideas about what the toll should be and shivered. "I say we make her show us her bosoms and let us all have a little taste of those sugar-sweet things."

Olivia heard them all laughing uproariously as

the leader, Mason, grabbed her again and ripped open her jacket and blouse. "I think that's a good idea." He laughed and reached around to pinch her tender nipples with both hands. "Line up, fellas, for a taste of our *sweet reward* here." They rushed around and over the barrels to get to Olivia and her exposed breasts. She squirmed to get out of Mason's grasp, but he held tight. Soon her breasts were being assaulted by the group. First one, then another sucked into his mouth a nipple of one breast and then the other while pinching the one he did not have in his mouth.

From behind her, Mason loosed his grasp and lifted her skirt. Olivia tried to kick at him as he tore her bloomers off and threw them over her head to his cheering cohorts. She had felt his erection through her clothing and now feared what his intentions for her were.

"We gonna get a taste of that too, Mason?" one of them called. "Just bend her over one of these barrels, and we can use her mouth too. No sense lettin' it all go to waste." Olivia felt them begin dragging her toward the barricade, hooting and laughing. She screamed and struggled, kicking at the closest men.

"Let me go, you ignorant, filthy swamp trash," Olivia yelled and bit into the ear of one of the attackers, drawing blood and a scream of pain.

"Son-of-a-bitch," he yelled. "The bitch just bit my ear off." He backhanded her, and Olivia saw bright pinpoints of light before her eyes. "That's what you do to a mare that bites," he said angrily and hit her again. Olivia sagged with the blow.

From behind, there came the loud blast from a firearm, and she was dropped to the ground as the men let her go to turn and see who'd fired the shot.

"Gentlemen, that's no way to treat a lady," Olivia

heard a male voice saying as she fell to her knees in the rough gravel. Though she was addled and dazed with shock, pain, and embarrassment, Olivia thought she recognized the voice of James Devaroe. Another blast from his gun sent the offending men scurrying for the hedges. "Wait a minute," he yelled to them, "move these barrels so we can pass."

"Aw, come on, friend," one of them whined. "We'll let you have a taste too. What's this pampered little cunny to you? We can all have a little of that sweet plantation-bred stuff."

Olivia heard another shot and the splintering of wood in the hedgerow. "The pampered little cunny just happens to be my wife, sir," she heard Devaroe say before she fell in a relieved faint to the gravel roadway.

She woke with her head resting on Devaroe's shoulder as they bounced along in the buggy down the road in the waning daylight. He pulled Blue to a halt when she lifted her head.

"I think we're probably clear of them now," he told her and got out of the buggy to light the lantern. "What in hell's name put the idea in your fool head to travel on the day the whole state was about to erupt into warfare?" he scolded her. "If I hadn't stopped by the townhouse to make certain you were alright and heard from Ben that you'd taken off for Sweet Rewards, God only knows what that lot would have done with you. I'm certain using your body for their pleasure would have been the least of it." He climbed back into the buggy and handed her the torn remnants of her jacket and blouse. "Do you honestly think they'd have left the daughter of Armand Thibodeaux alive to run home telling tales?"

With the realization of the situation, from which she'd just been rescued, Olivia broke down sobbing bitterly and clutching at the abdomen that housed her child. He left her that way for a while before finally wrapping an arm around her shoulders once more and pulling her close.

"Hush now, wife. You are safe, and I will see you safely home to your parents." That statement sent her into even more bitter sobbing. He stopped the buggy again. "Olivia, quiet yourself now. This caterwauling cannot be good for the child."

"What?" She sobbed. "What do you care about this child? You left us without support or care."

"I left you because you told me to go," he said sternly. "As for the support," he continued, urging Blue on once again along the dark track, "my banker insisted you had plenty in your private account to more than care for you and the child's needs for the time being."

"And it was fine with you that your child would be born in that part of town, surrounded by filth, drunks, and whores?"

"You are the one who chose the accommodations, wife. Not I."

"I am no longer your wife."

"As I told you before, when you first accepted my ring and accepted me into your bed as your betrothed, you became my wife in the eyes of God and the Church of Rome. I need no papers signed by magistrates or priests to claim you as a wife or this child as my legitimate heir."

"And if the child is only a girl and not a male heir?" She sobbed again. "Will you be like my father and treat her as a second-best prize?"

"I am not your father, Olivia. I will cherish a daughter just as I cherish her mother."

Olivia had no words to return and sat beside him quietly for the next two hours until they turned into the wide, tree-lined lane leading up to the mansion house of Sweet Rewards.

"Magdalena told me your mother is ill," he said as they neared the darkened house. "I'm sure she'll be happy to see you and hear our happy news."

"I am hoping it will give her a reason to hang on a little longer," Olivia said softly. "I want to put a grandchild into her arms before she passes."

"That would be a fine thing," he agreed and pulled the buggy to a halt before the wide porch with its tall white columns. "I see the light within," he told her and jumped down to bound up the stairs and knock on the door with its brass knocker.

❧ 25 ❧

"You are what?" asked Marie Thibodeaux of her daughter after being awakened by the noise in the foyer that brought her from her bed.

"I'm pregnant, Mother. I suspect the babe will come sometime in March if my approximations are correct, and I conceived on our betrothal night."

"Is that why you came back here? I wanted you to get away from here and have a good life in the city. I thought that was what you wanted as well, *Cherie.*"

"It was, Mother," Olivia said to her pale mother and laid a hand on her abdomen. "But I have another to think of now. I could not raise my child there. The neighborhood is not as it once was."

"So Georgia tells me. Magdalena has written. I had no idea things had changed so desperately."

"Yes, and with the political unrest, I thought it would be prudent to come back here now."

Marie touched the bruises on her daughter's face and frowned. "Perhaps not as prudent as you thought, *Nez pas?*"

"Perhaps not." She laughed weakly. "If it hadn't been for James..." Olivia closed her eyes and shuddered.

"Yes, we owe him for so very much." She smiled and patted her daughter's hand. "Your father is going to be so very pleased with this happy news."

"What happy news?" Armand Thibodeaux huffed as he came into the parlor, followed by James. "That this fool girl decided to come home for a visit when the State of Louisiana is about to declare war upon itself?"

"No, Armand." Marie silenced him with a smile. "The happy news is that you are going to be a grandfather."

"What?" he asked with his eyes wide and his brow furrowed in surprise.

"Yes, Father," Olivia said, looking past her father to Devaroe. "I am with child. I wanted to get out of the city *before* it exploded."

"And almost got yourself defiled and killed by Jerome Mason and his ridiculous crew of White Leaguers," her father growled. "I'll see that fool bastard and his lot hung for it."

"I'm fine, Father. There is no sense in muddying the waters when you know for a fact that all these fools out here will side with him. They are all afraid the Republicans are giving the Negroes too much power and that they'll have their throats slit in the middle of the night by their former slaves. Just let it go. James had them running with their tails tucked like whipped pups as it was."

Armand turned and slapped James Devaroe on the back with a broad smile on his scarred face. "Yes, it sounds like he certainly did, but I can still make life very hard for Mason and his pack of pups. We own a goodly portion of the banking company's shares, holding the mortgages on all their pitiful little farms. It will be a cold day in Hell before any of them get another extension of credit, and I will personally be presenting the eviction notices when any of them misses a payment." He gave Devaroe a sly smile. "Some of those properties border Sweet Rewards. If I buy up the paper on their loans, we can extend our holdings here some."

"My wife has a little money, Armand." Devaroe smiled. "Why don't you let her buy it up and serve the evictions?"

"Where would Olivia have gotten that kind of money?" Armand demanded. Olivia frowned at her unborn child's father and glanced toward her mother with a slight shake of her head.

"Where else would she get it? I gave it to her as a wedding gift," Devaroe said.

"Of course you did," Armand said, slapping him on his back again.

"Cherie," Marie said with a relieved sigh, "I must get back to my bed." She rose, and Olivia noted how weak her mother was. Armand put a supporting arm around his wife's waist, and Olivia was surprised to see what looked like an actual loving concern in her father's eyes.

Olivia took her husband's hand and led him to the stairs. "Are you ready to retire, husband?" she asked and squeezed his hand.

"Are you inviting me to join you in your chamber?" he asked her seriously as he followed. Halfway up the stairs, he stopped her. "Olivia, I will respect your wishes. If you do not want to continue with this marriage, I will not force the issue." He reached a hand to touch her belly. "But this is my child, and I will love and care for it as I promise to love and care for you."

Olivia laid a hand over his. "You have never uttered the word love to me before, James." She continued up the stairs. "I lust for you, that I do not deny, James, but I can't honestly say that I love you. Not like the love I had for William. I can't promise you that I ever will, but I will do my very best to be a good wife to you and a good mother to your children."

"Children?" he said quizzically.

Olivia smiled up into his face. "When Georgia examined me after we arrived and listened to my womb to make certain the attack had not injured the child…" She took a deep breath before continuing. "She is fairly certain she heard two heartbeats with her glass and says my womb is larger than it would normally be at this stage of pregnancy. She is certain I am carrying twins."

"Twins?" he gasped. "Twins!" James Devaroe swept her up in his arms and crushed her to him, kissing her passionately. "Yes, wife, I love you. I love you all." He beamed and pressed his hands to her belly. Together Mr. and Mrs. James Eduard Devaroe retired to their chamber on the second floor of the mansion house of Sweet Rewards to enjoy their joyous news and enjoy one another.

Dear reader,

We hope you enjoyed reading *Sweet Rewards*. Please take a moment to leave a review, even if it's a short one. Your opinion is important to us.

Discover more books by Lori Beasley Bradley at
    https://www.nextchapter.pub/authors/lori-beasley-bradley

Want to know when one of our books is free or discounted? Join the newsletter at
    http://eepurl.com/bqqB3H

Best regards,

Lori Beasley Bradley and the Next Chapter Team

ACKNOWLEDGMENTS

I'd like to thank Adam Sterling for pushing me to write a romance. I set in the Historic South where I'm more comfortable, but here it is. I know it's not the 'Classic Romance,' but I attempted to keep the story in tune with the times. Racial bias in the post-war deep south was rampant, and women had no rights, and women of color had even fewer. I wanted to write a story about two sisters separated by race but who loved one another despite it. Forgive me for the use of the 'N' word, but there wasn't much political correctness in the Jim Crow South, and I wanted the story to be true to the time.

Thank you to my critique group at HobNob's in Phoenix, The Central Phoenix Writers' Workshop. You guys have taught me so much!

Thanks to Wikipedia for all the historic fact-checking. I'd be lost without you.

Sweet Rewards
ISBN: 978-4-86750-403-1
Mass Market

Published by
Next Chapter
1-60-20 Minami-Otsuka
170-0005 Toshima-Ku, Tokyo
+818035793528

4th June 2021